A Heated Confrontation

Without thinking, the earl leaned in closer. "Then perhaps I shall steal a kiss."

"Do you always have to use a knife to purloin kisses from a female?" demanded his prisoner.

Alex gave a throaty chuckle. "No, usually they are all too happy to offer their charms without the need of such extreme measures. Indeed, I often must use a weapon to fend them off."

"Arrogant oaf." Aurora's eyes sparked with anger. "In my experience, most men use force to take what they want."

He drew back a touch, surprised at the undertone beneath the harsh retort. Was it a note of vulnerability? Fear, even? With a sudden start, he wrenched his mind away from such odd musings. What the devil had come over him? This was hardly the time to be flirting with a pretty young lady. Especially *this* lady.

His grip tightened on her arm. "Enough of games, sweeting. It's not money I seek, but information."

The Banished Bride

Andrea Pickens

A SIGNET BOOK

SIGNET
Published by New American Library, a division of
Penguin Putnam Inc., 375 Hudson Street,
New York, New York 10014, U.S.A.
Penguin Books Ltd, 80 Strand,
London WC2R 0RL, England
Penguin Books Australia Ltd, Ringwood,
Victoria, Australia
Penguin Books Canada Ltd, 10 Alcorn Avenue,
Toronto, Ontario, Canada M4V 3B2
Penguin Books (N.Z.) Ltd, 182–190 Wairau Road,
Auckland 10, New Zealand

Penguin Books Ltd, Registered Offices:
Harmondsworth, Middlesex, England

First published by Signet, an imprint of New American Library,
a division of Penguin Putnam Inc.

First Printing, March 2002
10 9 8 7 6 5 4 3 2 1

Chapter One

The dice hit the scarred wood with the rattle and crack of musket fire. A sharp howl followed, as if the dotted cubes of ivory had indeed dealt a mortal wound.

"May Lucifer be poxed. I'm done for!"

A rumble of drunken laughter greeted the slurred words.

"Aw, stop your infernal moanings and have another tipple, Woodbridge. It's still early and your luck is bound to come around."

The other gentlemen who were pressed cheek to jowl around the gaming table nodded while the one who had spoken groped for the large wad of vowels and shifted them a bit closer to his person. "Let's have another throw, but, say, at double the stakes this time—" The words dissolved in a loud belch and hiccup. Uncorking another bottle of port, he sloshed a generous amount in each of the empty glasses before him. "To make it interesting, I'll put up five thousand pounds against each of you in turn."

"Damn nip cheese of a pater won't spring for another farthing 'til next quarter day," groused a short, ginger-haired man whose bulbous nose was already threatening to eclipse the vivid color of his thinning locks.

"Your note is good 'til then, Hervey. What about the rest of you?"

The portly viscount seated to the right of Hervey took a moment to grope at the scantily dressed barmaid moving by his chair before nodding a quick assent. The gentleman to the left, his weasely face screwed in an even more furtive expression than usual, did the same.

"Belmont and Jarvis here have coffers as deep as Loch Ness," whined another of the group as he waved an unsteady hand at the other two. The burr of his Scottish accent was roughened by the goodly amount of whiskey he had consumed. "They can afford to match their blunt against yourn, but I'm rather strapped for the coin of the realm at the moment." He ran a careless hand over his disheveled cravat, already stained with sweat, and flicked the ash from a half-smoked cheroot off one of the sagging folds. "What say ye, Bull, will ye take some pledge aught than sterling?"

"Perhaps, MacAllister—if it's interesting enough." Baron Trumbull's bleary eyes became a tad more focused. "What do you have in mind?" he demanded.

The Scot leaned over and whispered something.

A meaty palm smacked against the rough wood, setting the dice to bouncing over its breadth. It was followed by a roar of laughter loud enough that for a moment it drowned out the babble of curses and slap of cards echoing through the murky confines of the gambling hell.

"The devil's ballocks, how can a man say no to that!" cried the baron, a lopsided leer tugging at his slack lips. "A bawdy house in Chigwell, you say? You are offering to put up a bawdy house as your stakes?"

"Aye. The girls be sturdy Scottish lasses." MacAllister

gave a sly wink. "From the Highlands, where they breed 'em for spirit and stamina, if that's ter yer taste, laddie."

"Oh, that's quite to my taste. You're on," he agreed, already licking his chops at the thought of what delectable dishes might be served up for his pleasure. When the lewd jests from the rest of his cronies finally petered out, he turned in some impatience to the last man of their party. "Well, what say you, Woodbridge. Will you stop your sniveling and join in as well?"

The earl drained his glass. "Mac ain't the only one with pockets empty of the ready. He ain't the only one with flesh to offer, either," he growled in a sulky mutter. A dribble of sticky spirits ran down his unshaven chin, but it went ignored as he sought to trump the grinning Scot. "I got an even better offer."

"Oh?" Trumbull leaned forward, nearly losing his balance and toppling from the rickety chair. "Pray, what could be better than a houseful of sluts?"

It took even longer for the shouts of inebriated laughter and risqué comments to die away.

Woodbridge bared his teeth in an attempt at a smile. "How about a husband for that troublesome chit of a daughter you are always complaining about? Think on it. Finally free of all family responsibilities. And you would be rid of the bother and expense of a Season, something you would be hard-pressed to avoid when she comes of age."

"Hmm. And just who do you propose for such a match?"

"My youngest son." Gratified by the gasps of surprise from the rest of the group, he went on with some smugness. "It's a good connection, for though he won't have the title, ours is a good family. You might do better, but not without a good deal more effort and expense on your part."

"Ain't the girl only a child, Bull?" asked Hervey.

"And a sharp-tongued little shrew, just like her mother. Anyway, fourteen ain't so young—"

The earl waved away the objection as well. "Aye, it's done all the time. Lock her back in the nursery for a few years, if need be."

Trumbull rubbed at his jaw. "What makes you think your son will be willing to go through with it?"

"Oh, he'll be willing, I promise you," answered Woodbridge, a nasty smirk slowly turning his expression even uglier. "I've got control over the one thing he wants, and to get it, he'll have to dance to my tune, for once." Under his breath he added, "And a merry jig I'll make him dance. Serve the impudent whelp right, after all the times he's flouted my authority over the years."

"Is he still a pup, then?"

"No, no, nineteen—or is it twenty? Can't keep track of the whole cursed litter of them."

The baron didn't hesitate more than a second or two. "Done. You're on as well, Woodbridge." He reached for the dice and caressed them between his fingers. "Come, gentlemen, let's play."

It was over rather quickly. Hervey scribbled out another vowel, while Belmont, Jarvis, and MacAllister each chortled over their winnings.

When it came to his turn, Woodbridge stared at the baron's toss of double sixes and simply shrugged. "Ain't many times when losing affords me nearly as much pleasure as winning," he muttered.

"Can't say I wouldn't have preferred a whore to a husband." Trumbull frowned. "But might as well make some use of the deal. Let's have the thing over and done with as soon as possible. I daresay in another two years she'll be your son's responsibility, not mine anymore."

Belmont cracked open a fresh bottle and poured another

round. "I say, how about a toast to the lucky couple and their prospect of wedded bliss."

That drew the biggest laugh of all.

The bride, swathed in a confection of white silk that was nearly three sizes too large for her tiny frame, was all but dwarfed by the bull of a man who led her down the aisle. It was well that size and strength were inarguably in his favor, for by the way the slip of a girl was dragging her feet, she looked ready to bolt if given half a chance.

The small church was empty save for the girl's governess and several of the groom's family.

The groom himself was nowhere to be seen.

"Damn it all, Woodbridge," growled Trumbull out of the corner of his mouth as he passed the front pew. "You promised me the fellow would show. If you've caused me to go to the trouble—"

"Ahem." The rector cleared his throat in mild rebuke at the baron's choice of language.

"There's nothing to worry about. He'll be here," answered Woodbridge, though his face betrayed a trifle less assurance than his nonchalant tone. His elbow dug into the ribs of the young man at his side. "What the devil is keeping them?" he whispered, ignoring the clergyman's baleful stare. "You said Harry had things well under control when you left them."

"He did, Father. I swear it. I can't imagine what—"

His words were interrupted by the creak of the heavy oak door being wrenched open, then falling shut with a resounding bang.

"Sorry for the delay," muttered the heir to the Woodbridge title, a young man whose thin, reedy build was in marked contrast to his father's bulging beefiness. "Dreadfully sorry," he repeated, trying to straighten the creased folds of his cravat with one hand while the other sought to keep the gentleman who was leaning against his left shoulder upright.

Neither attempt was overly successful. The starched linen refused to fall into any semblance of order, while his companion's knees folded all too neatly, threatening to send him sprawling on his face smack in the middle of the aisle. Harry Fenimore abandoned his struggles with the recalcitrant *trone d'amour* in favor of using two hands to right his listing sibling.

"Sorry," he intoned yet again, seemingly at a loss for anything better to say. The sound of their boots beat an erratic tattoo on the stone floor as the two of them tacked from side to side, narrowly missing coming to grief on more than one of the varnished pews. Finally the eldest Fenimore managed to straighten their steps and navigate a course toward the altar. With an audible sigh of relief, he drew his youngest brother to a dead stop.

By then it was evident to all that the groom was dead drunk.

"What are you waiting for, man? Get on with it!" ordered Trumbull through gritted teeth.

"Er, yes, of course, my lord." Goaded on by the sharp words, the rector appeared to be in as great a hurry as the baron to be done with the havey-cavey affair and sailed through the first part of the ceremony without lifting his eyes from the pages of his prayer book.

"Do you, ah, Elizabeth Jane Aurora take this man to be your lawfully wedded husband, to have and to hold, in sickness and in health, 'til death do you part?"

There was an ominous silence that lasted until Trumbull gave his daughter's arm a shake and whispered in her ear. The soft sound that then came out may or may not have been a "yes" but as the girl made no attempt to flee, the rector ignored such nuances and raced on.

The same question was asked of the groom. His response was a slurred "Why the hell not?"

That gave the clergyman some pause for thought. "Uh, I shall take that as a yes," he decided after a moment of hesitation. Then, without further ado, he decided to skip over the rest of the ceremony and simply mumbled, "I now pronounce you man and wife."

The book snapped shut

A pen was handed to the bride, who carefully wrote out her signature on the marriage lines in a neat copperplate script. The groom's fingers, guided in no small part by his brother's hand, scrawled what looked to be an illegible scribble. The witnesses then stepped forward to affix their names to the document as well, and the ceremony was at an end.

"Well, aren't you going to kiss your lovely bride, sir?" asked the rector, trying to inject a proper spirit into the odd proceedings while mopping at his brow with a large handkerchief.

James Hadley Alexander Fenimore took one look at the veiled child who was now his lawfully wedded wife, then turned away and was promptly sick in the urn of cut tulips and dahlias.

"Sorry," intoned his oldest brother.

Trumbull marched his daughter over to where her governess stood, white-lipped with silent anger. "Take her home," he muttered. "And stop glaring at me as if I were a naughty schoolboy."

"The birch rod should have been turned on your worthless hide years ago," she retorted.

The baron's face turned an angry shade of red. "Remember, two more years, then out onto the streets you go as well," he snarled. "And may you starve in the gutter for all I care, you meddlesome woman. If it weren't for the fact that the little hellion would raise more trouble than it's worth, I'd turn your sour face out far sooner than that."

"Unnatural man," said the governess, uncowed by his threats. "You are as monstrous a father as you were a husband."

He looked as if to speak, but then simply turned on his heel and stalked off to where Woodbridge and his sons were milling about in some uncertainty.

"I've arranged for a wedding breakfast at Trumbull Close before all of you head back to Town," he announced with a brittle joviality. His gaze ran over the gentlemen while speaking, and the forced smile slowly disappeared as he counted only three of them. "I say, where the devil is my daughter's husband? Can't have a proper wedding breakfast without the damn fellow."

All eyes turned on Harry Fenimore. He swallowed hard. "Ah, well, as to that, I'm afraid Alex is in a bit of a hurry." Before anyone could press him further on the matter, the groom reappeared from a side vestry, slightly more steady on his feet this time around.

The Earl of Woodbridge began to voice his displeasure but stopped short on seeing that his youngest son had already shrugged out of his coat of navy superfine and had the scarlet regimentals of a lieutenant in the Horse Guards draped over his broad shoulders. "So, I see you have wasted no time in purchasing your colors," he growled after a moment.

"I've kept my end of the bargain, Father." His lips curled up in undisguised contempt. "Knowing the value of your word, I took no chance that you might renege on the rest of the deal and had Perkins finish all the arrangements and the transfer of funds before I left Town."

"Ungrateful whelp," snarled the earl. "I should take a belt to your hide for such disrespect."

A slow smile played on Alex's rugged features as he

straightened to his full, not inconsiderable height. "Would you care to try it again, sir? As I recall, your last attempt resulted in a black eye and two broken ribs. Not mine, I might add, though I was a good deal smaller than you at the time."

His father choked down a curse but edged back a step.

"As for being ungrateful," continued Alex. "On the contrary, dear Pater, I am most thankful for the chance to put as much distance as possible between myself and your clutch-fisted attempts at tyranny. Indeed, my regiment sets sail for India tonight on the ebb tide."

"India!" sputtered Trumbull, his pudgy face growing pale with dismay. "Why, that's"—he had to close his eyes to think for a moment—"far away. Very far away. How long will you be gone?"

Alex shrugged. "I've no idea. The longer, the better."

"B-but your father promised you would take the chit off my hands when she turned sixteen."

"Did he?" He began to do up the row of polished gold buttons. "Then I suggest you discuss the matter with him. It's of no interest to me what you two scoundrels have arranged. I doubt I shall ever lay eyes on the girl again."

"But . . ." Trumbull's words trailed off as Alex moved behind a pew and stepped out of his pantaloons and dress pumps. Taking out a pair of buckskin breeches from the small valise he had brought in with him, he pulled them on and started to tuck in his shirt.

The baron tried another tack. "You have a responsibility to the girl! She's your wife, for God's sake—you can't just abandon her!"

"Can't I?" he replied coolly. "She is my wife in name only. As far as I'm concerned, I am as much a pawn in this grotesque game as she is. If you are so worried about her welfare, see to it yourself."

"Woodbridge!" he cried, a note of desperation creeping into his voice. "What about your promise?"

The earl shuffled from one foot to another. "I suppose we might pack her off to Rexford House. It's the smallest and most run-down of the Woodbridge lands. And the most isolated. It passed to Alex directly from his grandfather on his reaching majority." He pursed his lips. "Yes, that should answer for it. Trust me. She will be well out of your way there and won't be able to raise any trouble."

The baron looked somewhat placated. "You'll raise no fuss about such an arrangement, Fenimore?"

"None whatsoever." Alex tugged on his Hessians and straightened his collar. "I told you; do whatever you wish with her. I couldn't care less." Hoisting his valise in one hand, he made one last adjustment to his coat and started for the door. "Harry. Charles. Come walk me to my horse so that we may say a proper good-bye. God knows if or when I shall ever see England again."

Chapter Two

The young lady looked up from the letter she was writing. "What was that, Robbie?"

"I hate to disturb you when you are in the middle of your paperwork, especially as I know that Her Grace is being particularly demanding these days"—a loud sneeze interrupted her words— "but I'm afraid there is something that cannot wait."

Aurora Sprague looked up. Or, to be totally correct, Elizabeth Jane Aurora Fenimore looked up. But as she had always favored Aurora over the others, and had long ago discarded her married name for that of her mother's family, it was the moniker by which she was known.

"The crotchety old battle-ax may be particularly demanding, but she is also our best client." Aurora smiled and held up a leather purse that looked to be quite weighty. "Her Grace is also particularly pleased with the result of our last little investigation. This was just sent round and what I am struggling with is the composition of a particularly effusive thank-you note. If you can think of any really obsequious adjectives, I should be most grateful, for on that subject my vocabulary is decidedly weak." Her expression then became a good deal more serious. "But enough joking. What's wrong?"

Miss Edith Robertson mirrored her former charge's grave countenance. "Mary Tillson is downstairs. I think you had better come at once and see for yourself."

"Oh dear." She tossed her pen aside and pushed back from her desk. "Are the beatings getting worse, then?"

The older woman's lips thinned to a tight line. She nodded.

"Damnation," muttered Aurora under her breath. "We'll have to move faster than I had planned."

A thin young woman sat at the kitchen table, a piece of beefsteak being pressed up to her right eye by the cook. The purpling bruises on her nose were nearly as dark as the slab of meat and the split lip as raw.

"A tooth is knocked out, too, Mrs. Sprague," said the cook in a low voice. "I'd like to take a cleaver to the beast what done this. Chop off his hands, I would. And quite likely some other part of his anatomy as well. Then dice it all up, along with his lily liver, for mincemeat and—"

"I think we get your drift, Alice," murmured Aurora. "But I imagine Mary would rather not hear any further talk of spilling blood, even if it is her brute of a husband's." She stepped forward and put her own shawl around the woman's bony shoulders.

"I didn't do nuffink," sniffed Mary, as she brushed away a tear. "I swear, not even a w-word. But he came at me agin, jes the same."

"Of course you didn't do anything wrong. None of this is your fault. Not one bit." Aurora smoothed back a bit of the young woman's tangled hair from her wan brow, then pulled up a chair. "Is your aunt still willing for you to come to her in Scotland?"

Mary choked back a sob. "Yes. Mam wrote to her as ye

suggested, Mrs. Sprague, but what good is it? Will's drunk up every farthing we have, an' Mam can't spare a ha'penny, what with mill cutting back on hours." Another tear trickled into the hollow of her cheek. "I wuz hoping I might sleep on yer scullery floor ternight, and then borrow a shilling or two from ye te make me way te Lunnon."

"And what do you imagine will happen to you in London, Mary, without money or a place to stay?" asked Aurora gently.

The young woman hung her head. "Dunno, but it can't be worse than wot Will does te me."

"Well, it won't come to that. I told you that I meant to see you safely over the border as soon as I could afford it. And now I can, thanks to the fact that the Duke of Putney likes to tumble milkmaids in the Greek folly erected by his grandfather."

Mary blinked her one good eye in some confusion.

"Never mind," murmured Aurora. "Alice, please fix Mary some tea and see she has something hot to eat. Then take her up to the attic room. She should be safe enough there for a night or two. Naturally, if Mr. Tillson comes round to make any inquiries, we haven't seen his wife in weeks."

"What if he demands to come in and have a look around?"

Aurora smiled sweetly. "Why, then take a cleaver to him." She rose and gave one last hug to Mary's frail form. "Don't worry. I'll soon have you in Scotland where your husband will never touch you again."

"What would us wimmen do without ye, Mrs. Sprague? Yer a real angel sent down from heaven."

"Well, I suppose that depends on your perspective," said Aurora with a wry grin. "I imagine most men think I'm a devil sent up from the bowels of hell."

Miss Robertson grinned before another sneeze shook her ample frame.

"Oh, and Alice, while you're at it, better brew up one of your herbal tisanes for Robbie. She appears to be coming down with a nasty cold." There was a clatter of metal. "That is," added Aurora with a low chuckle, "if we might tear you away from your sharpening stone."

"No need for that. I'm really feeling quite fine," protested Miss Robertson, though her assertion was blunted somewhat by a flurry of hacking coughs.

"Go to bed, Robbie." With those parting words, Aurora turned and headed back to her study, already starting a mental checklist of all the things she must put in order if she were to be setting off on a long journey first thing in the morning.

Instead of following her former charge's orders, Miss Robertson waited several minutes, then marched after her.

"I thought I told you to get some rest," muttered Aurora, not looking up from her papers.

"Hmmph. I must be going deaf as well as blind." The former governess placed a pair of steel-rimmed spectacles on the bridge of her nose and picked up a dog-eared ledger from the corner of the desk, along with the duchess's bulging purse. Taking a seat on the faded chintz sofa, she set to work counting the coins and toting up the neatly penciled columns. "Hmmph," she repeated, this time with a positive inflection. "The Sprague Agency for Distressed Females has done rather well over the last two months." There was a brief pause while her eyes fell to running over the figures one last time, just to make sure everything added up correctly.

The Sprague Agency for Distressed Females. Aurora's mouth gave a mischievous twitch. She loved the utterly innocuous sound of the title. Most men, on hearing such a name, would assume she did nothing more than dole out vinaigrettes for flighty nerves or more exotic potions de-

signed to stimulate procreation. *Ha!* Little did they know
that her little hobby involved such things as assembling detailed dossiers on philandering husbands and analyzing financial information to see if a lady was being cheated out of
her rightful money. And, perhaps most importantly, giving
free advice, along with financial aid if needed, to poor
women who had no one else to turn to in order to help them
escape from under the thumb of tyrannical men.

The whole thing had started rather innocently enough several years ago. She had helped a neighbor—a *very* rich
widow—avoid the clutches of a smarmy fortune hunter by informing her of several rather indiscreet comments the gentleman had let fall during a night of drinking with his cronies at
a local tavern. Her smile broadened. It was truly amazing the
sorts of things gentlemen would say in front of people they
considered their inferiors or the incriminating evidence they
would leave lying about to be collected as trash.

Just the sorts of things that barmaids, tweenies, char-
women, and the like were happy to pass on to a person who
could put them to good use.

Naturally her neighbor had been enormously grateful and
demanded to express such sentiments in a material way.
Since Aurora and Miss Robertson relied on the former governess's modest inheritance as their main means of support,
the additional funds were quite welcome. Some months
later, the duchess asked if they might be of some help to a
bosom friend from school. The reclusive countess wished to
know whether the suitor for her daughter's hand was indeed
the paragon of perfection he seemed to be.

Soon, what the two of them still jokingly referred to as
The Sprague Agency for Distressed Females was nothing to
laugh at. Word of mouth had slowly spread throughout the
area that if a female had a problem, Mrs. Sprague and her
companion could be counted on for both sage advice and
sensible solutions, all dispensed with the utmost discretion.

The arrangement had suited Aurora perfectly, for not only was she poor, but a bit bored as well. After all, she had always possessed a keen intelligence, a practical mind and a skill for organization. Now she had a chance to exercise all three, as well as satisfying her sense of compassion. It didn't hurt that she knew firsthand what it was to suffer a gross injustice at the hands of the opposite sex. Such degree of empathy no doubt contributed to her rapport with those who sought her help, no matter what their station in life—

Another bout of coughing interrupted Aurora's musings. Struggling to suppress the nagging tickle that had crept back to her throat, Miss Robertson went on in a slightly raspy voice. "Yes, even without taking into account Her Grace's recent remuneration, we have turned a bit of a profit for the first time in ages."

"Well, there was that little matter of Mrs. Wilkes wondering how on earth the profits from her husband's tavern seemed to be draining away so quickly, like so many tankards of ale on a Saturday night." Aurora chewed on the end of her pen. "She was most grateful to learn about the mistress tucked away in High Wycombe. And then there was Mrs. Nevins, the dressmaker from Abingdon whose supplier was charging double the true cost of Chinese silk. We saw a handsome portion of what she saved, as I recall."

"We did." Miss Robertson paused to blow her nose. "And a good thing it was, because of late we have also had more than the usual number of requests for help from women like Mary, who cannot afford to pay even a modest fee."

"You surely would not have me turn them away."

"Of course not!" she sniffed. In an undertone she added, "Not that it would matter a whit if I did."

That brought a faint smile to Aurora's lips. "Am I that stubborn?"

"Let us say that most of the time you are quite sure what it is you want."

A duet of laughter, its harmony tuned by years of companionship, echoed through the cozy room. As the last notes died away, Aurora set aside her jottings and cupped her hand in her chin. "Well, I am quite sure that I want to help Mary. She is by far the worst off of our clients. Indeed, I even fear for her life if we don't act soon." Her fingers began to twist at one of the coppery curls that had escaped from the simple arrangement pulled back off her forehead. "I had hoped to pay off a number of back bills with our current windfall, but I suppose the butcher and the candlemaker can be convinced to wait a bit longer. The trip to Scotland cannot be put off, Robbie."

The other woman drummed her fingers on the open ledger. "We should be able to manage without having to resort to cold porridge and shoe leather." Sneaking a peek at her former charge, she added in a low voice, "And on the first of the month, we should be receiving the quarterly payment from Rexford. That will help tide us over."

As expected, the mere mention of the place brought a fiery light to the young lady's emerald eyes. "I would prefer it if we didn't have to touch a farthing of that dratted man's money."

"Why?" countered Miss Robertson. "I should say you deserve every bit of it for the monstrous wrong you have suffered." She drew in a deep breath. "At least he displayed a shred of decency in providing a modest stipend for you to live on, something neither your father nor his can be accused of possessing."

That was perhaps true, thought Aurora, though the admission was a grudging one. The dratted man—she refused to think of him as her husband—had sent word that as of her sixteenth birthday, the time designated for her removal to his estate, a small quarterly stipend would be forwarded to the village post nearest Rexford. And that, he had made quite clear, was to be the full extent of his attentions, both monetary and physical. 'Til death do them part.

Well, that suited her just fine. She didn't want his money. And she most certainly didn't want his—

"It was a stroke of luck that I found that letter crumpled up in your father's study," continued the former governess after a wheeze. "Else we should never have known of the arrangement. The fact that he bothered to send it before he embarked, however curt and unflattering the words, shows that of all the gentlemen involved in that shameful affair, he is perhaps the least reprehensible."

"That is hardly saying much." Aurora's lips had curled in some contempt, but the flames of her anger quickly died down, replaced by a spark of wry humor. "Though to be fair, I suppose I have to admit he *has* shown a shred of decency by staying half a world away from me. Just as I suppose I should be amused that after all these years, the money still arrives like clockwork. I can only assume that no one has ever bothered to inform him that I never showed up at his godforsaken estate." Another thought seemed to come to mind, one that lightened her expression even more. "Or perhaps he's had the decency to stick his spoon in the wall."

Miss Robertson tried to look stern, but the effect was ruined by yet another violent sneeze. "It is quite wrong to wish for anyone's demise."

"You're right—wishing rarely works. Maybe I could hire someone to do the job. In India there are certain sects—"

The other lady waggled a warning finger.

"Just joking."

Far from eliciting any chuckle from her former governess, Aurora's teasing words caused the older lady's hands to clasp together in her lap and a pained grimace to crease her brow. "I shall always regret that I was not able to protect you from such a horrible fate. But your cursed father gave me no warning. I was just as surprised as you when he demanded I dress you in your mother's old wedding gown and have you ready to depart for the church in ten minutes." There was a protracted sniffling, and not merely on account of the incipient cold. "Now here you are, a beautiful young lady robbed of the chance to fall in love and marry the man of your dreams—"

"Oh, come now, Robbie. There is no need for tears." Aurora's mouth hovered somewhere between a scowl and a smile. "Honestly, I think you must give over reading those books of Mrs. Radcliffe. It appears all the melodrama and nonsensical notions of romance are beginning to addle your usually unimpeachable reason." She let out a harried sigh. "You may be quite sure that even if I were free to do so, I would not have the slightest inclination to contemplate marriage."

"But you haven't had the chance to get to know a proper gentleman—"

"And why would I wish to do that? Gentlemen do not seem to have much to recommend them. Only look at the one I am leg-shackled to! Lord, it was a true godsend that you inherited Rose Cottage and the means to allow us to escape from my father's clutches. Otherwise I should merely have been exchanging one drunken lout for another." She shook her head vehemently. "Mark my words— I shall never, *ever*, seek another husband." Any hint of smile had long since faded. "Not that I sought the one I have now."

The sigh that filled the little room came from Miss Robertson's lips this time. "A shame he was not more worthy of regard, for the man was a most handsome devil, with those broad shoulders and thatch of dark hair." Then a most ungoverness titter escaped her lips. "Even if those long legs were a trifle unsteady."

"Unsteady? Why the man was by all accounts completely jug-bitten."

"Don't use cant, my dear. It isn't ladylike." Miss Robertson's voice quickly recovered its schoolroom decorum. Still, for all its proper tone she couldn't help but sneak in another question. "Do you not remember him at all?"

"I could barely see a dratted thing through all that gauze of my veil. Nor, if you will remember, was I tall enough to regard much more than the gentleman's waistcoat. Which was of an unobjectionable material, unlike my legal spouse."

Miss Robertson ran an eye the length of Aurora's willowy figure. "That's true," she said after a moment. "You did not shoot up to your present height until the following year. However, it cannot be said that your, er, husband isn't fashioned from good cloth when it comes to appearance. Simmy Cummings, who saw him ride off on his stallion, said he cut quite a dashing figure in his scarlet regimentals."

"I abhor the color red. It does not suit me," Aurora muttered under her breath as she twisted another errant strand of coppery hair around her finger. "Just as such sentimental rubbish is out of character for you, Robbie. You must be more ill than you think, to be waxing so girlishly romantic over a fellow we both know to be a jaded scoundrel."

The other lady's remonstrance was cut short by a hacking cough.

"That's it." Aurora crossed her arms. "I'll hear no more argument on the matter. You are taking to your bed this instant."

"B-but the journey to Scotland! I need to pack my bags and have —"

"The only journey you will be making is to your bedchamber."

"You cannot travel alone," protested Miss Robertson.

"I will not be alone," pointed out Aurora with unassailable logic. "Mary will be with me. And since it is perfectly acceptable for a lady to be traveling with her maid, propriety will be served. Not to speak of the fact that such a disguise will hide our friend's flight from any would-be pursuer."

"Still," croaked Miss Robertson, her voice becoming more gravelly by the moment, "if you would but wait a day or two, I'm sure I shall be fully recovered."

Aurora only rolled her eyes. "And pigs may fly," she murmured. "Seriously, Robbie, we don't have any time to spare. Despite Alice's dire threats, I doubt she and her cleaver would prove a match against Mary's brute of a husband should he take it into his head to search for her here. We must leave tomorrow." At the sight of her friend's crestfallen expression, she got up and went to drape an arm around the quivering shoulders. "The duchess has kindly offered me the use of one of her old carriages whenever I have need of it, and one of the under coachmen to go with it. I assure you, it will only be a long, boring, and tiresome trip that you are missing. If it is adventure and romance you are looking for, you had best stick to your horrid novels."

"Blimey, it's hot." The man wiped at the stream of sweat running down the bridge of his nose, then slapped at a fly buzzing around his wide-brimmed hat. "Hades could not be much worse, I imagine. At least we'd already be dead, and not constantly worrying about someone trying to put a period to our existence."

His companion chuckled. "This is merely a trifle warm, Fitz. Now, India—India was hot." He paused to shift the brass spyglass a fraction to the left, then motioned for the other man to duck lower among the tumble of boulders that concealed their presence. "Ah, just as I thought. Here they come," he whispered. "Stay down. I'm going to crawl out a bit farther on that ledge so I can be sure to get an accurate count."

The man's rough-spun garments were coated with enough dust and dried mud to blend in to the fallen scree and weathered rock as he slithered toward the edge of the overhang. Below, a troop of mounted French cavalry trotted by, followed by what looked to be a brigade of Spanish conscripts marching at a desultory pace, though their officers kept up a steady stream of harangues. It took some time for all the soldiers to pass, and even then, the two observers waited another quarter of an hour before retreating from their hiding place on the ridge.

"You were right again, Alex," said Captain Fitzherbert Battersley as he mopped at his brow with a dirty bandanna. "Marmont definitely appears to be shifting his men north. That's the fourth group in two days that we've observed on the move."

The other man nodded. "Aye, something's brewing." He ran a hand over the three-day stubble covering his chin. "I think we had best cut short the rest of this reconnaissance mission and report back to headquarters. Wellington should know of this without delay."

They picked their way back down the steep path until reaching the scrubby stand of cork trees where their horses were tethered. Checking to make sure both their pistols and rifles were properly primed and cocked, the two English officers mounted and rode off.

"Ah," sighed Captain Battersley as they trotted into camp some hours later. "I am looking forward to sluicing some of this damn grit from my delicate peaches-and-cream complexion, some measure of cover from the unrelenting sun, and a long swig of something wet—preferably good English ale rather than that thin red swill our allies call wine." There was a fraction of a pause. "Though not necessarily in that order."

Before his companion could frame a suitably pithy rejoinder, a young adjutant, his slightly bewildered expression betraying his recent arrival to the Peninsula, ran up and gave a tentative salute. "M-major Fenimore?"

The ensuing nod seemed to relieve a good deal of his anxiety. "The general ordered me to keep a close watch for your arrival, sir, but I wasn't quite sure I had the description right."

Battersley laughed. "You mean he told you to be on the lookout for a scruffy-looking devil with eyes the color of India sapphires and like as naught a dusky senorita in hot pursuit?"

The young officer blushed. "Well, sir, as to that—"

Taking pity on the young man's embarrassment, the major cut off his stutterings. "You said the general is looking for me?"

"Yes, sir." As if suddenly recalling the superior rank of the shabby figure before him, the newly arrived lieutenant threw back his shoulders and snapped to attention. "He said he wanted to see you the moment you rode in."

Alex gave a weary sigh. "No rest for the wicked, I see. It looks as if I shall have to wait to join you in draining that tankard of ale." He dismounted and tossed the reins of his stallion to his friend. "I'll meet up with you later."

"Ah, Fenimore," growled General Winthrop, looking up from a sheaf of dispatches as the major was ushered in. "Glad to see that once again, you have returned to us in one piece. I should loath losing one of my best officers on one of these damn dangerous reconnaissance missions you insist on taking part in."

"The lives saved are more than worth the risk of my own callused hide, sir. Besides, the Peninsula seems rather tame compared to the oppressive climate, rampant disease, and bloodthirsty sepoys of India."

The general motioned for him to take a seat at the folding camp table, then signaled for his orderly to pour two brandies and bring them over, along with the bottle. "Still, it appears that I *shall* be losing you, Fenimore." He raised the spirits halfway to his lips before adding, "I mean, Lord Woodbridge."

Alex's glass of brandy hung in midair. "*What* did you say?" he demanded in a hoarse whisper, though he was sure enough of his hearing to know he had not mistaken the words.

"I regret being the bearer of bad news, but it appears your brother Charles succumbed to a putrid throat some months past. This letter from Whitehall just arrived with the news." He pushed the wrinkled missive across the scarred wood. "Your man of affairs thinks it imperative that you sell out as soon as possible and return home to take up your responsibilities as the new Earl of Woodbridge. As does the War Department. They don't like the idea one bit that an old and respected title such as yours is threatened. After you, the next in line is some damned tobacco farmer from the former Colonies. Can't have that."

"Hell and damnation," growled Alex through clenched teeth. "But I don't *want* to sell out." Nor did he wish to be the earl, but it appeared he had as little choice in that matter as in his imminent departure from the army.

He stared at the spidery writing covering the travel-stained paper and muttered a few other choice obscenities under his breath. Never had he given a thought to the possibility of acceding to the title. Oh, his father's death some years ago from a bad liver had come as no surprise—the old reprobate had downed enough sauce in his day to pickle an entire regiment. Even when Harry, having inherited his father's taste for spirits, gave up the ghost in some foolish prank involving the racing of curricles along the cliffs of Dover, the succession had never seemed in doubt. Charles, his middle brother, had turned out to be a man of great sense, if not imagination, well content to spend the great majority of his time running the Woodbridge estates and attending to the myriad other responsibilities that came with the title. He had done a good job of it, too, restoring the lands to their former profitability and refilling the family coffers.

His tanned fingers laced through his dusty locks. However, it was a damn shame that Charles had not seen to the most basic of those obligations—namely taking a wife and producing an heir. In his letters, he had made vague mention of perhaps spending the next Season in Town in order to choose a bride, but in truth, Alex had come to the conclusion that the mere thought of a marriage ceremony had left his sibling quaking in his boots.

The general eyed him with some sympathy. "It is not always easy for us men of action to contemplate a more placid existence. But I daresay, you are a resourceful fellow, Woodbridge. You'll adjust."

Alex's mouth twisted downward in an expression that showed how little credence he gave to such assurances. "Sir, I wish to object—"

"Won't hear of it, Major, and that's an order. You are to leave at dawn for Lisbon."

The edge in the new earl's voice was as sharp as the jut of his jaw. *"Yes, sir."* He rose stiffly, hands clenched at his sides. "Then I had better go pack my things. Am I dismissed, sir?"

A weary sound, more snort than sigh, escaped from the general's lips as he motioned for his subordinate to be seated. "Come, finish your brandy, Major. You have plenty of time for that." His hand rubbed at his lined brow. "Can't for the life of me understand why it is you young sprigs prefer risking life and limb on the battlefield to waltzing at Almack's."

Alex downed his brandy in one gulp. "The lemonade at Almack's is notoriously weak. And the tongues of the Town gossips can flay the skin off a man's back as surely as any saber," he muttered, drawing a slight smile from his commanding officer. "Besides, I am hardly a young sprig anymore. I turned thirty several months ago."

"Then you are old enough to know better. It's time you stopped seeking danger in every corner of the globe and returned home."

"There has never been anything worth returning to," he growled.

"Well, there is now. My advice to you is to find a female you can have a regard for and settle down to the pleasures of married life. Take it from me. It's not half so bad as you fear. A compatible mate can become a true comrade in arms, one whose loyalty and love you will come to value above all things."

The new earl's face went rigid, and despite his tanned complexion, his color turned a shade paler.

"But enough philosophizing." The general's gnarled fingers drummed a light tattoo on the rough wood. He seemed to be deliberating on something, but after a long pause, he finally went on. "However, if you are truly so reluctant to give up the life of a soldier, there is one last mission you might undertake for your country before returning to London."

Alex's expression became a tad less bleak. "Sir?"

"A French courier was recently captured on a small bark that had set sail from Ayr, on the west coast of Scotland. He was carrying certain documents that lead us to believe vital information is making its way north from Whitehall across the border, where it is passed on to the enemy. A rather thorough interrogation of the man revealed little—except that the agent he dealt with is a female." He cleared his throat. "Given your considerable talent at ferreting out information, as well as your, er, no less considerable skills with the opposite sex, both Whitehall and I think you are the perfect man for the job. It would be of great service to us. That is, if you are willing."

The words were scarcely out of the general's mouth when Alex blurted out, "Of course I am willing, sir! In fact, I should be delighted."

A dry chuckle answered such enthusiasm. "Yes, I rather thought you might. Well, then, a fast mail packet is waiting in the Lisbon harbor." He paused to scribble an official order, then handed it over to Alex. "Give that to the sloop's captain. The boat will drop dispatches at Penzance, then continue on to Ayr and set you ashore. One of our local agents will meet you with any further instructions. The only other bit of information our informant could tell us was that the next exchange is set for three weeks from Saturday, in the village of Girvan, just down the coast from Ayr."

"Thank you, sir." If he could not change the inevitable, he thought with a last little grimace, he could at least put it off for a bit. Nearly overturning his chair in his haste to rise, Alex snapped a hurried salute. "It does not sound like it should prove much of a problem."

"Take care, Woodbridge," murmured the general. "Do not underestimate the peril you are walking into, just because you are stepping back on sovereign soil. Or because your opponent is a female. They can sometimes prove to be the most dangerous and cunning of all." He took a deep breath. "They can make a man react with emotion rather than reason."

The new earl's lip curled in some disdain. "Believe me, sir. I have long since been immune to the wiles or charms of any woman. I may bed them, but other than that, I have little use for the opposite sex. On the whole, they are greedy, grasping, manipulative harpies who think only of increasing their purse or their prestige through latching on to a gentleman. You have little reason to fear that my emotions—or my heart—will fall victim to a sultry smile or coy gaze."

Chapter Three

Aurora tucked an errant curl back up under her bonnet and surveyed the dimly lit public room. At this hour it was not the smoke but rather the grime that prevented more than a few wan rays of sunlight from penetrating the paned glass. Suppressing a grimace, she took another sip of her tea. At least most of the male travelers who had been present during the evening meal were far too hungover to be up so early.

If Robbie had not been so befuddled by illness, she reminded herself, the redoubtable former governess would likely have remembered the one key fact that both of them had overlooked in the haste to be off. To whit, while Mary had served as a proper companion on the journey north, once she was safely delivered to the cottage of her aunt, Aurora had been left to negotiate the trip home by herself.

She hadn't quite realized how tedious the ramifications could be, especially as her clothing was hardly of the first crack and her carriage a bit shabby for wear. The balding merchant from Dundee had been particularly hard to convince of the fact that his garlic-enhanced invitations to share sleeping arrangements were of no interest. It had taken a slight nudge on the narrow stairs to show him the error of his thinking. No doubt he would be nursing a sore rump as well as a splitting headache when he woke up.

Men, she fumed, her teaspoon stirring up the last of her lukewarm brew with a tad more force than necessary. They were more trouble than they were worth, that was for sure. Pushing aside the chipped plate of dry toast and watery marmalade, she stood up and went to pay for the meager repast, certain that the shot would prove to be as much of an outrage as the charge for a night spent between dingy sheets that couched a goodly number of live bodies other than her own.

Her carriage was waiting at the far end of the muddy yard, the driver looking none too happy at being rousted from the straw at first light. His mood turned even more sour as a few drops of rain fell from the leaden skies. As no one made any sign of coming to her assistance, Aurora reached up and tugged open the door.

How odd, she thought, pausing for a fraction to peer into the inky darkness. She could have sworn she had left the curtains tied back. Then, with a shrug, she placed her foot on the iron step and started to climb in. Her ascent was suddenly made all the more swift by strong fingers that wrapped around her wrist and jerked her inside. The door slammed shut and she found herself in a man's lap, a hand over her mouth and a blade of cold steel pressed up against her neck.

"Not a sound, sweeting, or I shall be forced to cut your throat." The knife pressed a bit harder, as if to emphasize the command. "And a shame it would be, for it looks to be a very pretty throat." It did indeed, added Alex to himself. *Too bad it is the throat of a traitor.*

Aurora leaned unresisting against his broad shoulder, making no attempt to cry out or to struggle.

"I see you have a modicum of sense to go along with your looks."

She jerked her knee up hard, hoping to catch him a solid blow to the groin. The maneuver almost worked, but his reflexes proved a tad too quick. He shifted just enough so that her effort merely glanced off his thigh.

"Ah, sweeting, to succeed in such a move, you must be sure that your opponent is truly off guard. You would have done better to distract me with a tear or two, then make the attempt." He reached up to rap a command for the driver to start off.

Twisting her mouth free from his grasp, she snapped, "I shall remember that, you lout." Her fingers sought to push away his arm, but it held her in a viselike grip. The sharp edge of steel pinched a bit deeper. "If it is money you seek, your judgment is as bad as your manners," she added. One of the curtains had been jostled during the short struggle and a bit of light filtered into the carriage. Aurora kicked up at the hem of her skirts. "My purse is as shabby as my dress. It will make but a meager prize." She then gave a slight sniff at the odor of cheap brandy clinging to the rough wool of his jacket and wrinkled her nose in disgust. "Though no doubt even a few shillings will keep you in good spirits for a day or two."

Lord, he had to admit, she was the one who had spirit. In spades. And courage to boot. But to do what she did, that should come as no surprise. She was a skilled and dangerous enemy. But still, he could not tear his gaze from the lush curves of her lips, now pursed in a delectable moue of anger. Without thinking, he leaned in closer. "Then perhaps I shall steal a kiss."

"Do you always have to use a knife to purloin kisses from a female?"

Alex gave a throaty chuckle. "No. Usually they are all too happy to offer their charms without the need of such extreme measures. Indeed, I often must use a weapon to fend them off."

"Arrogant oaf. In my experience, most men use force to take what they want."

He drew back a touch, surprised at the undertone beneath the harsh retort. Was it a note of vulnerability? Fear, even? With a sudden start, he wrenched his mind away from such odd musings. What the devil had come over him? he chided himself. His icy detachment and ruthless efficiency were legendary among his comrades. It was most unlike him to be distracted, even for a moment, from the business at hand. This was hardly the time to be flirting with a pretty young lady. Especially *this* lady.

His grip tightened on her arm. "Enough of games, sweeting. It's not money I seek, but information," he growled.

Even in the near darkness he could make out the sneer on her lips. "If that is the case, then it hardly makes sense to threaten slitting my throat."

A grim smile crept to his lips. "You have a certain raw courage, my dear, but the game is up." He shifted in his seat, trying to ease the stab of pain in his shoulder. Damn, the wound was beginning to bleed again. It had been most unfortunate that someone had evidently been alerted as to his arrival. The bullet had only narrowly missed its mark, but the fellow who had pulled the trigger would have no chance to try again. His corpse was already feeding the fish off Ailsa Crag. "Your accomplice is dead, you know, so why not make this easy on both of us—"

Aurora couldn't stifle a gasp. "You . . . you have hurt Robbie," she whispered.

"I'm afraid Robbie is lying in a watery grave—"

A blow to his jaw cut off any further words. Then her fists began to pound against his chest. "How *could* you harm a sweet, little old lady, you despicable beast!" she cried. "*I* am the one who runs the whole operation. If you wish to avenge yourself, do so on me!"

Alex managed to catch hold of her hands. "Little old lady? The person you sent to ambush me was most definitely *not* a little old lady. It is *he* who lies beneath a fathom of water."

"*I?* I sent no one to take a shot at you," she retorted. "Though considering how men treat their wives, it is no wonder that *someone* did."

Her words were making no sense. Fighting off another wave of nausea, Alex forced himself to concentrate. Of course. She was trying to confuse the issue, the little witch. He twisted her arm hard around behind her back, drawing a cry of pain. He had never manhandled a female before in his life, but his strength was ebbing and he needed some answers out of her. Fast. "Tell me about the operation," he snarled, giving the limb another hard tug. "And quickly. Otherwise you'll have a broken arm to show for your stubbornness. Who supplies your information?"

Aurora winced, but bit her lip to keep from crying out. "Very well." Her voice sought to maintain some measure of dignity. "It comes from a wide assortment of my female friends. Barmaids, tweenies, cooks, milkmaids, and the like. Gentlemen seem to think anyone beneath them lacks ears as well as feelings."

This was even more confusing than her earlier words, but he went doggedly on. "Then what?"

"Well, it's really not hard to put the facts together. Numbers leave a trail that anyone with half a brain can sort out. It just takes a little perseverance and common sense. And then, you gentlemen tend to act like rutting sheep when engaged in an illicit affair—all lathered action and frenzied motion, with little mind as to who may be observing your behavior."

Despite himself, Alex felt his jaw go slack. "And?"

"After I compile the dossiers, I turn them over to the wife—it usually is a husband I have investigated, though on occasion it may be some other smarmy male relative—or whoever has requested the information." She drew in a deep breath. "Which aggrieved husband or uncle are you?"

He had the oddest sensation that the inside of the carriage was starting to spin. "What the devil are you talking about!" he shouted, wondering why his voice was sounding so fuzzy.

"Why . . . the Sprague Agency for Distressed Females. Isn't that what you are asking about?"

"Bloody hell! What in the name of Lucifer is the Sprague Agency for—" The knife suddenly clattered to the carriage floor, joined a moment later by the Earl of Woodbridge's lanky form.

"Bloody hell is right," muttered Aurora as she sought to lever the gentleman back up to the seat. He was heavier than he looked, for despite the obvious lack of padding around certain areas of his anatomy, he appeared to be all whipcord muscle wherever her hands touched. Ignoring the odd flicker of heat that the touch of him stirred within her, she wrapped her arms around his torso. For a moment, she was tempted to pry open the door and boot him out into the mud. It was what he deserved, the bosky fool. Lord, he must be well and truly foxed, first to accost her with a weapon, then to spout off with those addled rantings, and finally to pass out cold at her feet.

Men, she thought with a derisive snort, finally squaring his shoulders up against the squabs. It was then that she noticed the dark stain seeping through the tear in his jacket. Her fingers brushed over the rough wool and came away covered with a sticky red substance. For a moment she could only stare at the tangible evidence that his harsh accusations were not simply the working of a jug-bitten mind. Then, with brusque efficiency, she peeled the outer garment down from the wound and turned to find her reticule.

Mixed in among an assortment of useful items was a small flask of brandy. It had already proven quite handy on several occasions during the journey, for somehow, her driver had always proved more willing to go on until the next inn after a wee nip or two. Uncorking its contents, Aurora shifted closer to the man's unconscious form. A jolt of the carriage threw her up against his side, and a hard object poked into her ribs. She swallowed hard then felt gingerly at the pocket of his jacket. Her fingers withdrew a large and very deadly looking pistol. To her unpracticed eye it appeared to be primed and cocked.

Her mouth twitched in a grim smile as she placed it next to the knife she had retrieved from the floor. *We shall see who is in the position to be making threats,* she thought to herself with some smugness. She brought the flask to the man's mouth and forced a few drops down his throat. The rest she dumped over the wound on his shoulder.

"OUCH!" He sat up with such force that Aurora was nearly knocked off the seat. She sidled back across the worn leather and took up the knife in one hand and the pistol in the other. After all, she still had no idea of what he was doing in her carriage. Was he a thief? An enraged spouse? Or merely a madman?

His eyes fluttered open. On catching a glimpse of the weapons pointed in his direction, they fell closed again and a string of oaths tripped from his tongue.

"Really, sir, there is no call to be so vulgar. In case you have forgotten it was *you* who accosted me, and not the other way around."

He shifted slightly, causing a sharp intake of breath. "Damn," he murmured. "Weak as a kitten." One lid pried open, and Aurora couldn't help but notice the color that was revealed was blue. Not just an ordinary blue, but a brilliant sapphire. How was it she hadn't noticed before?

"Go ahead and pull the trigger," he continued raggedly. "Doesn't matter. Whitehall knows about you. Will send another in my stead."

She searched her memory. Whitehall? She had made no probings into the affairs of any such fellow. "You must be mistaken, sir. I don't know him."

A humorless laugh answered her words. "Your skills are such that they must rival those of the famous Mrs. Siddons, though I've yet to see her tread the boards. But you may leave off your role of confused innocent. We know where the French are getting such information."

It suddenly dawned on her. Whitehall. *That* Whitehall. "For God's sake, you think I am a . . . spy? A spy *and* a traitor?"

His lips curled up in a mocking half smile.

"Hell's teeth, I *should* shoot you. Of all the nasty, unfair things I have been called by various gentlemen, I vow that is truly the worst. Not to speak of being too idiotic for words. You must be the most bumbling British agent in all of Christendom."

The second eyelid popped open, along with his mouth.

"Really," fumed Aurora, before he could get a word in edgewise. "It is outside of enough that anyone—much less anyone who is supposed to have an iota of intelligence— would think that I was capable of betraying my country. To begin with, I've never been within a hundred and fifty miles of London and Whitehall in my life. Just how am I supposed to hatch my nefarious schemes at home in—well, in a small village? A home that contains such dastardly accomplices as an aged cook, an ex-governess, and a housekeeper whose gouty knees keep her from climbing up and down the stairs more than twice a day. Then, of course, there is the calico

cat, six chickens, one swayback cart horse, and a milk cow."
She shook her head in disgust. "Truly a band of dangerous
criminals that should strike fear in the heart of the British
government."

Beads of sweat seemed to be forming on the man's brow
as he shifted uncomfortably on the seat, but whether it was
from a fever brought on by his wound or some other cause,
Aurora couldn't tell.

"Er . . . The only thing I was told was that the enemy I
am searching for is a female. . . ."

"Oh, well that narrows down the field considerably," she
retorted acidly. "What did you do? Flip a coin to decide
which one to attack first?"

"You were traveling alone. Seemed rather havey-cavey."

"I wouldn't have been traveling alone if Robbie—that is,
Miss Robertson—hadn't taken ill at the last moment. Of
course, I had Mary with me on the trip north, but once I delivered her to her aunt, I was left without a female companion." Her chin rose a fraction. "I'll have you know I usually
plan things much better than this, but time was of the
essence, and sometimes one is forced to improvise." There
was a slight pause. "And furthermore, if I was a foreign
agent, I should hardly be seeking to draw attention to myself
by acting in an, as you say, havey-cavey manner."

Despite the pallor under his tanned skin, a flush of red
spread over his face. "I suppose that makes a bit of sense,"
he allowed. "Perhaps I might have been a bit hasty in—"
Another jolt of the wheel caused him to grimace in pain. The
beading on his forehead had changed to small rivulets running down his unshaven cheeks.

With a sigh of exasperation, Aurora set aside the pistol
and reached out to smooth away his tangled locks and touch
his skin. "Lord, you are burning up." Digging into her reticule, she took out a crumpled handkerchief and began to
mop at his brow.

"Don't suppose you have another flask hidden away in there?" he asked in a hoarse whisper. "Feeling devilishly thirsty." Before she could answer, he slumped against her shoulder.

"Oh dear, are you going to faint again?"

"I'm a soldier, not one of your distressed females," he mumbled. "Soldiers do not faint."

"No. They simply pass out," she remarked, taking care to lie his lifeless form across the full length of the cushion. Shifting to the facing seat, she rapped on the trap and called out to the driver. "Ranley, we must stop at the next cheap inn."

Alex awoke with a fuzzy head and the bitter taste of laudanum on his lips. He wished he might dismiss his recent memories as mere drug-induced hallucinations, but he knew they were all too real. He winced, not from the pain of his wounded shoulder but from the realization of what a cake he had made of himself. Over the years he had carried out a score of more difficult and dangerous missions, always with resounding success. Now, on his last assignment, he had bungled things badly, and in a matchup against an inexperienced country chit no less. What had she called him—the most bumbling British agent in all of Christendom?

He winced again. Lord, maybe the general was right, he thought glumly. Maybe he was getting too old for this.

A slight swish of skirts caused his eyes to come open.

"Oh, yer awake, sir!" The female sitting in a straight-backed chair by his narrow bed jumped to her feet rather nervously. Though she looked to be not a day under sixty, she moved toward the door with surprising alacrity. "I'll go fetch yer wife."

Wife? He must be dreaming—or rather, experiencing his worst nightmare.

"I see the laudanum is finally wearing off." The face that bent close to his was nothing like a nightmare. Indeed, he had forgotten how attractive she was, with those smoky emerald eyes and a cascade of curls. The shimmering color reminded him of exotic spice, while their texture looked to be as soft as the finest India silk. And that odd mouth, strong and a trifle wider than might be thought pretty, yet softly rounded, just as a woman's curves should be.

". . . back in the morning."

He blinked, realizing he hadn't heard a word she had been saying.

"Still groggy I see." Aurora pulled the chair closer to the iron bedstead and sat down. Her fingers brushed against his forehead. "But the fever seems to have passed. It's a good thing you have a strong constitution, for the doctor said a nasty inflammation had set in."

"How long have I been abed?"

"Two days."

"Two days! The devil—" He tried to sit up, but the movement caused him to feel a bit light-headed.

Aurora reached over and tucked the flimsy pillow behind his shoulders. "Perhaps that will help. I've also ordered up a bowl of porridge and some tea. You'll likely feel a bit better once you've gotten some food into you."

"Thank you," he muttered, his eyes avoiding hers. Lord, he was still appearing the helpless fool and it didn't sit well at all. "How did I get here?" he demanded after a pause, his voice a bit rougher than he'd intended.

"Do you wish the full account, or an abbreviated version?"

His brow furrowed.

"Actually, you had better hear it all, since you will have to stick to your part of the story if you wish to avoid drawing attention to yourself. Which, as a British soldier on a clandestine mission, I assume you do not. Even innocent country chits know that."

Alex could only nod, though his teeth set on edge.

"Very well." She rearranged the folds of her skirts, revealing, just for an instant, a very nicely turned ankle. He forced his eyes shut so that he might pay attention to her words. "I ordered my carriage to stop at the first inn that looked to be a bit . . . less patronized than some of the others. Informing the proprietor that my husband had been taken suddenly ill, I had my driver carry you up to this room, then engaged a second chamber with the explanation that I didn't wish to disturb your rest. The added blunt made it unlikely they would ask any further questions. A doctor was recommended, and after a certain number of guineas changed hands, he was more than willing to forget he had to dig a bullet out of your shoulder. We both agreed the inflammation and fever must have been caused by a putrid boil." Noting the reproachful look that crossed his features, she shrugged. "Well, we had to explain the bandages around your shoulder." Picking up where she had left off, she finished the story without further ado. "I also hired the innkeeper's mother and wife to help keep watch over you at night, thereby further ensuring their cooperation as well as avoiding being in the same chamber with a strange man. Oh, and as my purse is, as I told you, rather light these days, I took the liberty of paying for all this with the gold I found sewn in the lining of your jacket."

Alex was rendered speechless for a moment. Sweet Jesus, he thought, Wellington had found a rival for decisive action and deft maneuvering.

"Since it was likely issued by dear Whitehall, I figured I was entitled to it as well," she quipped. "We spies are known to get paid by both sides on occasion."

"Sorry," he growled. "If you recall, I was feeling a bit ill."

"Yes, no doubt the fever had addled your brain," she agreed. "There is no other explanation for such a patently ridiculous notion." Despite the edge of sarcasm to her voice, he noted that the line of her jaw seemed to soften somewhat. "So, you do not still think I am the dastardly spy you seek?"

"I suppose not. You have had plenty of opportunity to send me to my Maker."

"Hardly an overwhelming vote of confidence." However, her lips twitched in a slight smile, and he found he couldn't help but grin back.

"Thank you. For everything," he repeated softly. "Truly. I am usually not quite so cowhanded as this. Indeed, I haven't made such a hash of an encounter since—well, since I was much younger."

"No, I don't imagine you have." Alex was gratified to see her smile grow even more pronounced. "In your line of work I doubt you'd be around long if you had."

The arrival of the tray of food interrupted any further conversation. "Well, good night, sir. I shall see you in the morning."

As she walked toward the door, Alex tried not to stare at the sway of her slim hips. Indeed, he tried to put her out of his mind altogether. Waving away the elderly woman who had brought him his meal, he sat up by himself and began to attack the thick porridge. But his thoughts kept straying back to his rescuer.

Strong-willed females were usually not at all to his taste, he mused, chewing slowly on the crunchy nuggets. They inevitably proved to be demanding, greedy, and selfish to boot. But this young lady was intriguingly different. Why, most any other lady would have swooned at having a knife placed to her throat, but she had kept her wits about her, showing a feisty courage and an agile mind.

Too agile! he thought with a wry purse of his lips. Egad, had a female really disarmed him? He could only hope no word of that little encounter would ever leak out. First of all, his fellow officers would never believe it. And if they did become convinced of its truth, they would laugh themselves sick, no matter that he had been half delirious with fever. He would join in, he admitted, for the irony of a seasoned veteran being bested by a poor country miss was not lost on him. He had always been able to laugh at himself. It was what helped keep him sane over the years.

With a start, he realized he was chuckling aloud. *Damn!* Green chit she may be, but she had handled what could have been a disaster of epic proportions with cool aplomb and quick thinking. Lord, her concise report would have been a credit to any officer on Wellington's staff. He added *organized, smart,* and *savvy* to the growing list of her attributes.

As he shifted against the ragged pillow, he caught the faint lingering of her scent, a combination of lavender and warm honey. *Attractive.* Damn attractive, especially as it seemed clear she was no longer the enemy. Even when he had thought her thus, he couldn't help but be drawn into the hidden depths that lurked in those flickering green eyes. They looked to hold more mysteries than any exotic jungle.

And likely were just as dangerous, he chided himself. Lord, he must still be suffering the effect of the fever and the drugs. He hadn't reacted this way to a female since . . . He paused to think. Since never. The spoon rattled against the chipped bowl. It was simple lust, that was all. Lust made oddly edgy by the strange circumstances.

Of course, as a gentleman he would control such base urges, for he had never been one to prey on young innocents. And he would also see her reputation didn't suffer for her involvement with him. It shouldn't be too difficult to cover up the fact that they had spent several nights unchaperoned at a public inn. No one need know. He would see her safely to the main road to the border, before continuing on his own mission. Satisfied that he had thought of everything, he set aside the tray and blew out the single candle. His head had nearly settled against the pillow when an oath slipped from his lips. Then another.

Hell's teeth! It suddenly occurred to him that he didn't even know her name!

Aurora tugged on her nightrail and slipped between the scratchy sheets. She should be exhausted, having spent half the previous night tending to the feverish stranger and a good part of the day arranging for the doctor and medicines. Not to speak of convincing the rather suspicious innkeeper that nothing too havey-cavey was going on upstairs in his dusty little chambers.

Yet sleep was proving elusive. She turned on her side, then onto her back. No doubt she should have shoved the dratted man from the carriage at the first opportunity. Why, he was no different from most males—odious, overbearing, and smugly sure he was right, even when logic and fact dared contradict such opinion.

So why, every time she closed her eyes, did she picture blue eyes as mesmerizing as any jewel and a crooked smile that gave the hard planes of the unshaven face a boyish charm. Even those stubbly black whiskers had captured her imagination. They had looked to be so intriguingly different from anything she had ever felt, that, to her acute embarrassment, she hadn't been able to refrain from running her hand along the line of his jaw several times while he had been sleeping.

Nor had her gaze been able to keep from straying over the muscles of his chest, so contoured and so utterly different from her own gently rounded curves. Of course she had known men were different. She just hadn't realized quite how different, having never seen a man's bare chest at such close range before. There was hair, for one thing. Soft, curling wisps that had been surprisingly silky beneath her fingers. Her cheeks grew hot as she was forced to admit that yes, she touched them as well.

It was only natural that she had been curious, she told herself, defiant bravado seeking to silence her own uncertainties. After all, it seemed highly unlikely she would ever get this close to a naked—or near naked—man again in her life, so she had better make the most of it. . . .

The landlord had been convinced, for the outrageous sum of a guinea, to part with an old nightshirt. For another few shillings he had consented to put it on the unconscious soldier. It was too short and too wide for him, exposing a good deal of long, hairy leg. The fact that it was of thin cotton exposed something else—that below the unbuttoned front of the garment, he was also very . . . male.

Aurora was not quite a green girl. The distressed women she dealt with were graphically frank about the goings-on between the sexes, so there was probably not much that she hadn't heard, though, to be honest, some of it seemed to defy the laws of logic or physics. Still, it was hard to imagine that, well, a man could become any . . . bigger.

She rolled over and punched at the pillow, hoping to fight off such strange musings, as well as the disturbing tingle that seemed to be spreading out from her very core. It was not as if she was sorry that she would never be pressed up against a broad chest peppered with dark hair. Or that she would never feel muscled legs entwined with hers. Or that she would never be filled with the seed that might give her a child.

And she was certainly not sorry that she had never been kissed. She would have punched the rogue if he had leaned a fraction closer. Instead, she punched the pillow yet again to knock out all thoughts of a pair of glittering sapphire eyes.

Hell's teeth! It suddenly occurred to her that she didn't even know his name!

Chapter Four

A slight jiggling of the iron door latch brought Alex instantly awake. Cursing himself for not having taken the precaution of turning the lock, he rolled from the narrow mattress and landed lightly on his feet. Though weak, his legs at least felt steady, and his mind was no longer fuzzed with fever and painkillers. The pale moonlight showed the blade of a knife probing, testing to see if any latch was fastened on the inside. Then the sliver of steel disappeared and the hinges gave a tiny creak as a cloaked figure slipped into the room.

Alex made a lunge at the outstretched hand that held the knife, hoping to use the element of surprise to make up for his diminished strength. The weapon did indeed go clattering across the planked floor, but the intruder shook off his hand as if it were no more bothersome than a small terrier.

"Ah, Major Fenimore," came a low voice, muffled by several layers of a dark scarf. "Or should I say, Lord Woodbridge. You are proving to be a difficult fellow to shove into the grave."

"I have always disliked being bullied, especially by craven cowards. My father might have told you that had he not floated himself across the River Styx on a bottle of brandy. But perhaps you may follow and ask him yourself— you and your cohort who is now serving as sustenance for the crabs off the Isle of Arran."

What might have been a laugh sounded from within the cloth. "You may find me a bit more adept than poor Horton. You saved me a bullet, getting rid of the incompetent fool. But now I intend to finish the job he was paid to do." The intruder dropped into a fighter's crouch, feinting left, then right, in an attempt to force the earl to retreat a step or two. There was little space to maneuver in the cramped room, and Alex knew he could not afford to be cornered, for with his injury he would be no match for the other man in hand-to-hand combat. No, he would have to use guile to fight his way out of this.

His gaze swept the room. The window was too far away. But if he could edge toward the door, he might be able to escape down the stairs and elude any pursuit. A stoneware pitcher on the small table by his bedside was the last thing his eyes came to. He grabbed it up and in one motion flung it at the intruder's midriff. It doubled him over for an instant, just long enough for Alex to make a lunge for the opening. However, the other man was quick enough to recover and lash out with a booted foot. The blow caught him hard on the side of the knee just as he reached the half-open door, knocking him to the floor. By rolling to one side, Alex managed to avoid another nasty kick, then regained his feet, though now he was farther than before from any means of escape.

In India he had learned a number of tricks for self-defense that depended on technique rather than strength. When his assailant came at him, the earl took hold of the other man's elbow, and in a blur of spinning limbs, flung him against the iron bedstead. There was a growl of pain, a muttered oath, and then the intruder came at him again, this time a bit more cautiously.

"Oh! I-I thought you might be having a nightmare." Aurora was framed in the doorway, her wrapper pulled tightly round her willowy form, a thick plait of hair hanging down over one shoulder.

Another low laugh. "It appears your reputation with the ladies is not unfounded. I see you have wasted no time in finding someone to . . . minister to your needs."

"Nice little piece, isn't she?" Alex showed his teeth, hoping they wouldn't be knocked down his throat by the newest entrant to the fray. "Now sweeting, go back to your room. I don't have need of you just yet. But when you return, bring your friend, why don't you? She's got some flint to her, despite her rather long nose." He didn't dare take his eyes from his adversary, but he hoped the message was clear enough. The young lady had shown no lack of wits up to this point.

There was the barest of pauses. "Whatever you wish, sir. After all, you are the one paying for everything."

He certainly was, he thought, rubbing at his wounded shoulder. A pound of flesh had already been extracted, aside from the guineas that had been spent. The Lord only knew what price he would have to pay for implying she was a doxie, on top of having accused her of being a traitor and a spy.

"You're right—you won't have need of her where you are going, but I might fancy a tumble when I'm finished with you. Her driver informs me the chit is a long way from home, and quite alone now that her companion has stayed behind with a relative. No doubt she could use a . . . protector to fend off any unwanted attentions."

Damnation. Alex swore to himself. It was his fault the young lady had been dragged into this dangerous affair.

Now he would have to make sure that not only her reputation but her person emerged unscathed.

A moment later, she reappeared, the long snout of the pistol silhouetted against the white of her wrapper. "I take it you wish to, er, caress my friend Manton first, sir?"

Alex couldn't help but grin. "Hand her over—but I owe you a kiss, sweeting."

The sound of breaking glass shattered the stillness. One more kick cleared the shards and splinters enough for the cloaked figure to slip through the broken window and drop to the ground below. By the time Alex reached the sill, the dark shape had already crossed the yard and disappeared into the copse of trees.

He turned back, ready to be roundly castigated for his ungentlemanly words. Recalling her earlier outrage at having her patriotism called into question, he winced to think of how she might react to such an insult to her virtue.

A giggle was, therefore, not what he expected. Yet a giggle was all such a burbling sound could properly be called. Hand over her mouth, she sought to stifle the worst of it.

One of his brows arched in question.

"S-sorry. It's just that"—another whoop cut off her words for a moment—"that you look very funny, with your great, hairy legs sticking out of that ridiculous sack of a nightshirt."

Alex looked down. The garment barely reached his knees and was wider than the topsail of a thirty-gun frigate. With the breeze coming in from the smashed window, it threatened to sail even higher. He had to suppress a laugh of his own, though in truth, he was beginning to tire of appearing a bumbling nodcock in her eyes. First she had sneered at his intelligence. And now? It was a new—and unsettling— feeling to have a female reduced to giggles at the sight of him in a bedroom.

He had better start showing to better advantage, he decided, else the next thing she was going to start questioning was his manhood. Which was soon going to be on full display if he didn't don his breeches in short order.

In two strides he was by her side, hand clamped around her arm. "You may laugh all you like, but later. Right now you have three minutes to dress and gather your things." Propelling her out the door, he added, "After that, whether you are clad or unclad, we are leaving."

"But—"

"No arguments!" It was the tone he used with new recruits, the one that caused knees to quake and nervous fingers to check that every button was done up. "You are only wasting your seconds." His head ducked close to her ear and the tantalizing scent of lavender clinging to the sinuous braid that fell across one breast. Somehow, he couldn't resist murmuring, "I should prefer the latter, but it is up to you."

The spark of molten fire that flashed in her eyes was no surprise. But the fact that her jaw clamped shut and she did as she was told was a small miracle. Perhaps he was making some headway, despite his great hairy legs.

Funny, other ladies had found his long legs particularly attractive.

Following his own orders, Alex grabbed up his clothes from the chair in the corner, noticing that not only were his breeches freshly laundered but somehow she had managed to procure a new shirt, unsullied by blood or bullet holes. The jacket had also been replaced with one that did not smell as if it had been doused with a keg of ale. Lord, was there nothing the young lady could not accomplish with frightening efficiency?

Certainly her speed in dressing could not be faulted. Just as his knuckles were about to rap on her door, she appeared—fully clothed, he noted with a twinge of regret—with her small valise done up and by her side. Oh, a few buttons had been missed, and the high collar of her gown was slightly askew, but other than that, she looked eminently presentable. *Too presentable.* Behind her, in the shadows of her tiny chamber, the bed was a rumple of sheets, and he found himself wanting nothing so much as to lay her down upon their languorous folds and bestow the promised kiss. And then another and another, until she was not laughing at his legs anymore but gasping his name in sweet moans as he drank in the honeyed taste of her mouth, her throat, her—

"I thought we were in a hurry."

His eyes jerked up from where they had been fastened on the swell of her bosom and hint of nipple showing through the dark muslin. "Right," he rasped, his throat unaccountably dry. Taking up her bag in one hand and her arm in the other, he hurried their steps down the stairs and to the front door.

"The window—" she began.

He tossed a coin on the floor. "That should cover it, seeing as they have no doubt charged a king's ransom for everything else."

Outside, the first light of dawn was just beginning to seep above the gray horizon. "I don't think Ranley is going to be happy with being rousted at this hour—"

Again Alex cut her short. "You may leave that to me. I shall manage to convince him that it's time to be off," he replied softly, though the steel of command was once more evident in his voice.

She stared at him queerly for a moment, then merely nodded and followed along to the stable without further comment. In a matter of minutes, the driver stumbled out of the tack room, shirttails still hanging down, bits of straw clinging to his matted locks, and began shaking out the traces with more alacrity than Aurora had seen from the man in the entire trip. The horses were also led out and harnessed without delay.

"Come. In you go." Alex assisted her up, letting his hand linger on her arm for a fraction longer than necessary. He climbed in as well, and rapped on the trap for them to be off.

It was chilly inside, a cold made more raw by the threat of rain that glowered down from the scudding clouds. Aurora shivered as she leaned back against the damp leather of the squabs, for the light pelisse over her muslin gown added little warmth.

Alex couldn't help but note the slight tremor out of the corner of his eye, just as he noted that she bore her discomfort without complaint. He took the bundle that had been under his arm and shook it out. The blanket was hardly luxurious, but its scratchy wool would add some measure of warmth.

"I imagine we paid for it several times over," he murmured, leaning close to tuck it around her shoulders. "So your conscience, as well as your limbs, may rest easy."

Her eyes flew up with a start. Surprise rippled their emerald depths, along with a current of some other emotion he couldn't quite fathom. "T-thank you," she whispered.

The dark smudges under her eyes and the fine lines of strain pulling at the corners of her lovely mouth were unmistakable at such close distance. A wave of guilt washed over him. Lord, she had shown such grit and courage, he had forgotten how young and inexperienced she truly was. The string of silent curses he heaped upon himself was rather lengthy as he brushed an errant wisp from her cheek. "Tired?"

"Mmm. Just a little." Her lids were already half closed.

"Get some sleep. It will be at least an hour before we stop."

Her chin had already fallen forward onto the top of the blanket. In repose, her profile softened from that of warrior queen to one more resembling a simple young country miss, untested in the sort of battle he had dragged her into. Ignor-

ing the pain in his shoulder, Alex pulled her closer, so that
her cheek came to rest on his chest.

He couldn't resist taking a lock of her hair between his
thumb and forefinger, marveling at how even the dim light
picked out highlights ranging from rosy blond to deep cin-
namon. The colors reminded him of curry. A dish not to ev-
eryone's taste, but for those who could stand up to its heat,
its spice, its subtle complexities, it made all others seem
rather bland.

"Hmmph." She snuggled even closer, the soft zephyr of
her breathing blowing warm through the folds of his shirt
and feathering against his bare skin. Another gurgled sigh
and she curled her legs up against his thigh.

Lord, she may need his heat, but if she kept touching
him like that he was soon going to have to stop the carriage!
A good dousing in the heavy rain that had begun pelting
down upon the roof might serve to dampen the rather ungentlemanly thoughts that were starting to flare up in his
head.

But it was truly a singular sensation, he thought, not
knowing whether to gnash his teeth in frustration or chuckle
in bemusement. He had never before reacted to a woman in
quite this way. Oh, to be sure, he ached to undress her, to explore every tantalizing curve until not one of her marvelous
secrets was left unbared to him.

Yet his urges went beyond mere pleasure. He found himself wanting to keep her enfolded in his arms, safe from the
perils of the stormy world outside. His jaw tightened at recalling the cloaked intruder's casual crudeness. The thought
of anyone else touching her lit a different sort of spark in
his innards—the desire to commit murder with his bare
hands.

Where was such romantic nonsense coming from?

Any tender sentiments had long ago been beaten out of
him. After all, he had discovered quite early that it was

pointless to look for love or support from any of those around him. So he had learned to be harder than his father's fists, more resilient than a birch rod, and tougher than a leather strap. Instead of knuckling under, like his older brothers, the youngest Fenimore had been stubbornly determined to survive on his own terms.

He had done it, but at a cost. For while he expected nothing from anyone, in turn he'd had nothing to give. Perhaps that cold detachment was what made him such an effective soldier. *And such a rotten husband.* But that was a subject he had, over the years, taken great pains not to dwell on.

Feelings made one vulnerable. And being vulnerable was the one thing he feared above all else. The thought of exposing life and limb to any threat, even death, caused not a blink of an eye. The thought of exposing his heart . . .

With a shake of his head, Alex leaned back and closed his eyes, determined to marshal his wayward musings back into orderly ranks. He had started this whole mission badly, having made a number of silly mistakes that even the rawest recruit would have avoided. Lord, perhaps the general was right and he was getting too old, his edge too dull, if he found himself lowering his defenses for a managing country miss who had tumbled into his life by mere happenstance.

It was time to regroup. Time to reinforce the barricades around what was left of his tattered soul. *That* he would never surrender.

"Hmmph." Aurora shifted slightly. The pillow seemed to have a life of its own, for it moved, too. When she tried to knead out the lumps, it spoke as well.

"Easy, sweeting. I've taken enough punishment these last few days without you adding to the various bruises."

She blinked her eyes open, only to find her cheek was up against the crook of his shoulder, her hands splayed in intimate abandon across his chest. "Oh!" Her body would have shot upright had his arms allowed such freedom.

"Nay, sleep a bit longer. I'm sure you could use the rest."

"But—" Her mouth was parted in protest when his lips came down on hers. For a moment she was too overwhelmed to think of struggling. Though she had tried on more than one occasion to imagine what a man's kiss might feel like, no unschooled fantasy had quite prepared her for the visceral reality of it.

His mouth was firm, yet pliant, the rasp of his unshaven cheek on her skin only serving to counterpoint the silky glide of his lips over hers. But it was the things his tongue was doing that had her feeling as if the carriage had suddenly veered off the beaten path and plunged over a precipice. She reeled as it entered her mouth, plundering her senses with reckless abandon. He tasted of sea salt and foaming waves, and she found herself wanting to drown in the current he was creating inside her. Robbed of breath, she felt the vortex pulling her under. And the strange thing was, she didn't seem to mind.

It took a second or two for her to shake off the odd torpor and realize that he had set her back against the squabs.

She slowly sucked in a lungful of air. "I-I should slap you for such impertinence."

His sapphire eyes glinted with humor. "Surely your sense of honor wouldn't let you strike a helpless invalid."

"Helpless—ha," she muttered. "You appear to be quite recovered, sir, judging by the way you tossed your attacker through the air as if he were no more substantial than a sack of potatoes." She gave a slight tug to her bodice on noticing the disarray. On second thought, she decided she would much rather discuss what had happened back at the inn than the more recent grapplings. "Er, just how did you accomplish such a feat?"

He looked amused by her attempt to change the subject. "Mayhap I am not quite as bumbling as you think, sweeting." His lips came a bit closer. "And mayhap I'll take another kiss, since I have just given the one I promised."

Aurora shrank back, the pull of self-preservation winning out over the desire to throw herself back into the maelstrom. "Yes—it is my experience that most men simply take what they want. By force if necessary!"

The grin disappeared as he regarded her intently, and the laughing blue of his eyes clouded to a deeper hue. Then his shoulders settled back against the worn leather of the seat. "It's clear you have not been kissed with great regularity—"

"Hmmph!" She squared her shoulders. "I'll have you know I-I am a married woman!"

She was gratified to see that her announcement caused a pinch of surprise to spasm across his features. It was gone in an instant, replaced by what looked to be a rakish smirk. "What kind of husband allows his wife to gallivant across the length of Britain, without so much as a single servant to look after her reputation?" In a softer voice he added, "Or her virtue."

"The kind who isn't around to give a damn!" she snapped. "And if he were, I'd not let some arrogant, jug-bitten male dictate what I could and could not do, simply by virtue of his . . . plumbing rather than his brains!"

After the bark of laughter had died away, his face took on a serious mien. "A drunk, is he? Did he leave you? Or did you decide—"

"I don't wish to discuss my husband, sir! Not with you, not with *anyone!*" Aurora hoped her voice didn't sound quite so brittle to his ear as it did to her own. "The particulars of my personal life are none of your concern." She took a deep breath to steady her tone. "Besides, I'm perfectly capable of taking care of myself."

Save for the creak of the joints and the rattle of the wheels, an awkward silence filled the carriage. Her mood was not improved by the discovery that two buttons on the front of her dress were undone, showing a good deal more of her undergarment than she had realized. Muttering a word more appropriate coming from the mouth of a grizzled soldier than a young lady, she fumbled with the fastenings.

"You are quite right," he replied after some moments, a nonchalant shrug punctuating how little care he had for the matter. "Let us agree that neither of us has any call to pester the other with prying questions."

"Yes, let us," she said stiffly. Though, she added to herself, he could have been a bit more gallant about the whole thing.

"There is, however, just one further question that I wish to ask."

Aurora eyed him warily. "Which is?"

"Your name, madam."

"Oh!" She bit at her lip. "I suppose that makes some practical sense. It is Mrs. Sprague. Aurora Sprague."

"Aurora Sprague," he repeated slowly.

Funny, on his tongue it sounded alluringly exotic, like a warm tropical rain blowing through palm fronds, rather than just a gargled mouthful of hot soup. It made her feel, well, it made her feel a bit heated all over. To hide the flush of color rising to her cheeks, she turned to stare out the window. "And yours, sir?"

"Wood . . . more. Major Alex Woodmore."

Of all the cursed luck! Another scarlet coat to plague her dreams. "Well, Major, now that you have recovered sufficient strength to, er, fend for yourself, I imagine you will want to get back to ferreting out your spy. That is, assuming you are still convinced it isn't me." She gave a twitch to the blanket. "Is there a specific rendezvous point where we may drop you, or will the nearest place where you may procure a horse do?"

"I'm afraid things are not going to prove quite so simple, Mrs. Sprague. Unlike a cockleburr caught on your hem, I am not going to be quite so easy to brush off."

Aurora started. "W-what do you mean, sir?"

"I take it you are aware that last night's visitor was not making a social call—"

"Hmmph!" She interrupted him with a loud snort, then fixed him with a scathing glare. How dare the insufferable man speak to her in such a condescending manner! Why, if it hadn't been for her quick thinking and common sense his carcass might well be moldering somewhere out on the moors. "Oh, you mean to tell me he wasn't a friend of yours? Good gracious, I should *never* have figured it out on my own."

His lips twitched. "Don't fly up in the boughs. I was not implying any lack of intelligence on your part. Rather, what I was going to add was that our nocturnal visitor knew far more about our . . . identities than we might wish."

"What of it?" she muttered.

"Come now, Mrs. Sprague. I expect you to be quicker than that. What I am saying is, it appears he knows who you are and where you are headed."

"So? I am no threat to him. I know nothing."

"He is not likely to believe that. No, until I can be sure of your safety, you are not going anywhere on your own. I have a place where you can stay hidden, out of trouble, until I have dealt with this matter."

Aurora put on her most intimidating scowl, the one she saved for when the local rector was spouting some particularly irritating homily on the duties of females. "Since I don't recall ever having taken the king's shilling, I don't consider myself under your command, Major Woodmore. Furthermore, I am not used to *any* man giving me orders, so I suggest you get ready to dismount at the next stop. *I* am going on to the border." As a finishing flourish, she folded her arms across her chest and allowed her jaw a defiant little tilt. That, she thought with a sniff of satisfaction, should wipe the arrogant expression off the overbearing officer's face.

It did nothing of the kind. If anything, the man's lips took on a more pronounced curve upward. "Yes, it's quite clear you are used to doing whatever you wish, regardless of the risks involved," he murmured. "Your husband should be flogged for dereliction of duty, but it seems someone needs to take you in hand." In a louder voice, he sought to explain his decision. "This is for your own good—"

Aurora's reticule hit the other side of the cab with a resounding bang, and what appeared to be the sound of breaking glass. "I cannot stand it when men say that!" Her mouth was quivering with fury. "Of all the patronizing drivel! What you *really* mean is that it suits *your* needs. And since you cannot marshal any sort of rational argument, you resort to platitudes to excuse your tyranny." Playing what she considered to be her trump card, she demanded, "Give me *one* good reason to do as you say!"

The challenge didn't even provoke the slightest bit of hesitation. "One? Well, odds are quite good that he will have you followed and abducted." He paused. "Oh, but why stop with just one, when the possibilities are so tantalizing? Once in his clutches, he will subject you to a variety of unpleasant tortures to learn if you are telling the truth. Then, most certainly, he shall kill you." Alex then leaned back and laced his hands behind his head. "Oh, did I leave out the part about rape? As I recall, he did mention he fancied a tumble with you."

Aurora swallowed hard. It was galling enough that his

logic was unassailable, but did the dratted man really have to look so smug about it?

"The carriage must be returned to its owner," she grumbled after some moments. "And Robbie will be worried about me."

"I had already planned to send the driver on, since we need a more inconspicuous means of travel. He can deliver a note to your friend."

Aurora refused to look him in the eye. "So, you truly mean to hold me prisoner?"

"I shall try to refrain from using whips and chains."

She swore she could detect a note of laughter in his voice, and it goaded her to further retort. "If you try to force me into another kiss, I vow I shall not submit without a real fight."

He smiled, a twinkle lighting the sapphire depths of his eyes. "I consider myself forewarned, Mrs. Sprague. But no matter what you think, I am not completely lacking in honor. The next time I kiss you, it will be because you have asked me to."

"Ha!" Aurora made a point of turning her back on him and sidling as far into the opposite corner as possible without actually hanging out of the window. "And pigs may fly!"

Alex regarded the rigid set of her shoulders and nearly chuckled aloud. He could almost feel a twinge of sympathy for the man who had taken her to wife, for undoubtedly the poor fellow had gotten way more than he had bargained for. But then the humor slowly faded from his lips. He hadn't missed the blink of hurt in the young lady's eyes when she had spoken of her wayward spouse, though she had taken great pains to disguise such feelings. Shifting against the squabs, he found that his booted foot itched to come into contact with the fellow's posterior for bringing such an expression to her face. It might be true that he had never encountered such stubborn willfulness or feisty spirit in a female. And yet, he admitted after giving pause for thought, never had he met with such gritty courage or quick wits.

A man would have to be a bloody fool not to recognize what a rare—

He was the bloody fool, he chastised himself. And it was his own tail that deserved a swift kick for letting his thoughts stray back to such sentimental claptrap. This was no Arthurian epic and he was hardly her knight in shining armor. Not with his own tarnished past.

A harsh rasp escaped his lips. He should be breathing a sigh of relief at having discovered she was a married woman, not one of regret. Innocent young misses, with their flighty romantic notions and impossible expectations, had never held any attraction for him. A practiced courtesan or bored wife—that was the sort of jaded partner he preferred for dalliance. One who expected only his body, not his soul, and was satisfied with the pleasure he gave in the bed-chamber.

For that was all he had to give.

Instead of having to worry about protecting the intriguing Mrs. Sprague, he could, in good conscience, attempt a seduction. She was fair game. She knew the rules. Indeed, she appeared to flout them.

And yet, somehow the notion didn't sit quite right. It was hard to catch a glimpse of it, but at her core there was an innocence that belied the cynicism she chose to wrap around her like an ill-fitting cloak. There was a mystery to her and to the reason of why a man would abandon such unique beauty and spirit.

Why, if he had a chance to start over, he might consider—

No. He would not allow himself to think in that way. Ever the pragmatic soldier, he knew it was bad strategy to spend time pining over past mistakes. Better to get ready for the next battle.

His eyes strayed back to the mass of curls glinting with fiery highlights. And no doubt it would come sooner than later.

Chapter Five

The horse slowed to a shuffling walk without much urging from its rider and took its time skirting a tall stand of gorse, careful to avoid the tangle of thorny leaves.

"Mrs. Sprague?" Alex looked around in some consternation. He was sure he had not erred in finding his way back to where he had left her an hour earlier. Surely the headstrong young lady had too much sense to set off for the border on foot, despite her obvious displeasure with having her own plans summarily changed. His voice rose a notch higher. "Mrs. Sprague?"

There was a faint rustling of leaves, then what sounded suspiciously like an oath. The top of Aurora's head appeared from behind a drywall, followed by much heaving and scrabbling before the rest of her came into view.

He had to repress a chuckle as she swiped at the bits of thistle and hay that clung to her hair. "When I said to lay low, I did not mean for you to take it quite so literally."

A curl fell over her cheek. "It's all very well for you to laugh, sir," she replied with some indignation. "But I was only following *your* orders. A shepherd was approaching with his flock, and as you said it was best to remain out of sight, I made to duck behind the wall. How was I supposed to know there was a rather deep drainage ditch running the length of it?"

"Well, there is an old adage—look before you leap." She looked, Alex decided, ready to leap down his throat if he continued with such teasing. So, much as he enjoyed the way her green eyes turned to molten jade when she was angry, he left off trying to provoke her. Dismounting, he went to fish out her valise from the overgrown whin and brambles.

"Yes, well, I should definitely have looked before I leaped into my carriage the other day," she muttered. "I would have avoided a great deal of bother had I done so."

"I am cut to the quick to think you are not enjoying my scintillating company." He grinned. "Most females do, you know."

"Somehow, I doubt the wound will prove mortal to your vanity, Major Woodmore," she retorted. "Am I really supposed to be impressed with your irresistible charm and polish? So far, I have been accosted with a knife, forced to nurse my delirious assailant, then dragged from my bed by another deadly attack and made to flee in the dead of night." Aurora crossed her arms and scowled. "Robbie would be thrilled, for she dotes on Mrs. Radcliffe's novels, but I am not."

His lips twitched. "No? What happened to the starry-eyed notions of romance that every young lady secretly entertains, no matter her avowals to the contrary?"

There was a brief silence, broken only by the harsh cawing of a solitary raven. "Marriage happened," she finally answered, her voice as tight as the fists that were clenched at her sides. "And real life. Storybook romance has no place in such a world." She brushed away another wisp of hair that the wind had loosened. "Shouldn't we be moving on, Major Woodmore?"

Alex's expression sobered considerably. "Right." He moved to tie her bag behind the saddle, alongside his own meager possessions, but found it hard to drag his thoughts away from the conundrum she presented. It was difficult to reconcile the hardened cynicism of her words with the look of achingly youthful—almost waiflike—vulnerability that she tried so hard to cover with her scowls and frowns. Had the past really been so wretched as to strip her of fanciful dreams? Of—

". . . able to find no other mount?" Aurora stared at the nag he had secured from the run-down inn.

He head came round at her pointed inquiry. "There was little choice," he explained. "Besides, it was best not to attract undue attention by asking for two horses. With any luck, our adversary will think that you have managed to give both of us the slip." He fastened a last knot. "Don't worry, we don't have far to go."

"Surely you cannot mean to—"

His hands went around her waist as she spoke and swung her up across the pommel with ease. He spent a moment arranging the folds of her skirts, then found the stirrup with his boot and mounted as well.

"Major Woodmore," she began again.

"Mrs. Sprague, a clandestine mission such as this one demands that I keep my true identity a secret. It would be best if you did not continue to use that name."

"I can see the sense of that." She paused. "What would you have me call you then, sir?"

"Alex will do nicely."

"I hardly think—"

"After all," he reasoned, not without a mischievous grin, "we have gotten to be on rather intimate terms, having seen each other in various stages of undress over the past few days."

Her shoulders stiffened. "That is *not* very gentlemanly of you to bring up," she snapped. "Still, I suppose that what you suggest is acceptable, given the circumstances." Pulling away from his person as much as her awkward position would allow, she added, "However, it does *not* mean that I consider us . . . friends."

"No, of course not, Aurora," he murmured, drawing her rigid back closer to his chest.

"Insufferable man," she said through clenched teeth, but the shambling gait of the nag made it impossible to resist without resorting to an undignified squirming. Instead, she clamped her jaw shut and fell into a stony silence.

For a time, the only sounds were the dull thud of the horse's hooves on the damp earth and the swish of the tall grasses against its flanks. After a mile or so, Alex turned their direction from following the rough cart path and struck out for the top of a rocky knoll.

"Where are we going?" Aurora finally demanded, curiosity winning out over her resolve to ignore her companion.

Alex didn't answer, but spurred the animal into a semblance of a trot. Once they had crested the rise, he paused for a moment to survey the area, then gave a tug to the reins, urging their mount down into a small valley that looked to be nothing more than a sliver of overgrown pastureland cut out from the thick forest of oak and evergreens. The splash of water over stones soon revealed the presence of a small river skirting the edge of the woods as the animal picked its way through the thistles and thorns. It wasn't until they had descended to its banks that a small thatched-roof stone cottage became discernible up ahead, its weathered gray hue nearly melding into the outcropping of granite that stood in its lee.

Drawing the pistol from his coat pocket, Alex slid from

the saddle and lifted Aurora to the ground as well. "Stay here," he ordered in a low whisper, then moved off with quick but noiseless steps toward the low structure. In a matter of moments, he had disappeared around the far corner.

His movements became much more deliberate as he edged the wall, his back pressed up against the damp stone. The rough-planked door was firmly shut and the lack of any smoke curling up from the chimney seemed to indicate the place was utterly deserted. He stopped long enough to sound three short whistles.

The same signal echoed back to him from within the cottage. After a moment, the door swung half open. "The Peninsula is hot," said a low voice.

"But not as hot as London these past few months," replied Alex.

A figure slipped out from the darkened interior. "Ah, Major Fenimore—that is, Lord Woodbridge. I had expected you rather earlier." The man's pistol was still at the ready as he shot a look over Alex's shoulder. "Where is Urquehart?"

"Dead." Alex dropped his own weapon to his side. "Along with the fellow who set the ambush."

The other man frowned. "Damnation. What happened?"

"I'll explain in a bit. But first let me fetch my horse."

"You can tether him behind the rocks, along with mine. It's well out of the view of any casual observer. By the way, sir, I'm Wheatley."

Alex acknowledged the introduction with a curt nod. "I've heard a good word about you from the general. You're Sedgewick's son—the one who helped pluck Captain Hinchley from the coast of Brittany. A neat piece of work."

The younger man dipped his head in awkward acknowledgment. "Rather it is you whose exploits are legendary, my lord. I look forward to working with a man of your experience and ability."

Ha! thought Alex to himself with a wry grimace. *Not in a moment you won't.*

He was, however, a bit more circumspect when he spoke aloud. "There has, I'm afraid, been a bit of a complication added to the original plan. I do have someone with me, though not the man either you or I expected." Before Wheatley could voice the question that was forming on his lips, Alex finished off in a rush. "I'll explain that later as well, but it would be . . . safer for the person in question if our real identities remain a secret, in case of any trouble. There is to be no mention of Woodbridge or Fenimore. Just call me Alex."

The man nodded in understanding. "Very good, sir. Then I imagine I am to be simply Jack."

"Right. Now I'd best go get her." Under his breath he added, "Before she takes it into her lovely head to make off with my mount."

"Her!" exclaimed the other man in disbelief, but the earl was already around the corner.

"Hell's teeth." Jack couldn't help but mutter an involuntary oath under his breath on seeing the willowy figure clad in skirts duck through the door.

"Pleased to make your acquaintance as well," retorted Aurora, her chin lifting a fraction. "You may be sure, sir, I am no more pleased with the situation than you are."

Unaware that his words were quite so audible, the agent from London had the grace to color. "Er, I did not mean, that is, I—"

Aurora ignored his stammering. With a toss of her head, she undid the strings of her bonnet and shook out her curls, causing the man's words to become even more jumbled. Her eyes raked over the small wooden table, the bare earthen floor, and several wooden crates, then fell back on Alex.

"Now what?"

She could swear she detected a glint of amusement in his

eyes, though his expression remained impassive. "I'm sure you would like to rest for a bit," he said smoothly. "No doubt there is a pallet of some sort in the other room where you might lie down, is there not, Jack?"

"Er, yes. Though it's hardly the sort of thing fit for a . . . lady," croaked Jack. "I did not expect—"

"Nor did I," interrupted Aurora dryly. "I'm sure it will do." She reached for her valise before Alex could pick it up, and stalked to the flimsy door that divided the already small space in half. "I take your hint, sir, that the presence of a mere female is deemed unnecessary, now that there are serious matters to discuss." There was no mistaking the edge of sarcasm undercutting her words. "Well, it is to be hoped that *two* male brains will be sufficient to come up with a suitable plan." Her tone, however, indicated she wasn't betting on it.

"Good Lord," breathed Jack, wiping at his forehead with the sleeve of his jacket once the door fell shut with a rather loud bang. "Who in the name of Hades is *that?*"

"*That,*" replied Alex with a twitch of his lips, "is Mrs. Aurora Sprague."

The other man gave him a look that bordered on reproach. "I have heard whispers of your, er, reputation with the ladies, sir, but—"

"The redoubtable Mrs. Sprague has offered up not her virtue, but her timely assistance. Without her help I would likely not be alive." He then went on to explain all that had happened since his landing near the town of Ayr.

Jack gave a low whistle when the account was finished. "So they knew when and where you were coming, as well as your exact identity." He shook his head and his expression became very grim. "Things are even worse than we imagined. There are only a handful of men who knew all of that information. And I would have been willing to bet my life on it that they all were above suspicion."

Alex rubbed at his jaw but said nothing.

"The devil take it," continued Jack, giving vent to his frustration with the low oath. "It makes no sense. Each of them has an exemplary record in the service of his country."

"No debts or gambling losses or other such pressures that might drive a man to desperate acts?" asked Alex.

"That occurred to me also, but I turned up no hint of anything amiss in any of their personal affairs." His boot scuffed at the dirt floor. "There is something else deucedly confusing in this whole affair. Why he would trust a female to carry out the most important—and dangerous—part of the—"

"Of course it is difficult for you to fathom." Aurora closed the door behind her and breezed past them. "However, if you were to stop thinking in such a predictable pattern and used a bit of imagination, the answer would appear rather logical. At least it does to me." Secretly enjoying the startled looks her comment had brought to their faces, she paused to sweep the room with her gaze. "Is there any water here, or must I go fetch it from the stream?"

Jack nearly knocked over the crate on which he was sitting in his haste to retrieve an earthenware jug from his leather rucksack.

Aurora observed that while he was not so tall or broad in the shoulders as the major, he moved with the same lithe grace. Noting the ripple of muscle under the linen of his shirt, and the quickness of his movements, she decided to reserve judgment as to whether he was really quite as inept as first impression seemed to indicate. After all, he would not be the first male to have his wits momentarily addled by having a female speak to him as an equal. The question was whether he would be smart enough to listen.

With that in mind, she slanted another quick look at his face from under her lashes. There was no question it was a handsome one. No doubt he had a good deal of experience in amatory exploits, if not missions of a more serious nature. He had lively eyes as well—not, perhaps, as lively as the major's, but ones that hinted at a certain depth of intelligence. She decided to give him a chance to show his mettle.

"Well, at least you have managed to think of a few essentials," she allowed. When it became clear that no glass was to be forthcoming, she took a small swig right from the jug.

"Sorry," mumbled Jack, a dull flush creeping over his cheeks. "But I didn't expect—"

"Yes, yes, I know." Putting the container down on the table with a thump, she couldn't resist adding a further comment, in a voice just loud enough to be heard. "Really! If the fate of nations is in the hands of the likes of you two, it is no wonder that Bonaparte rules most of Europe."

The younger man turned rather green around the gills, but Alex gave a loud chuckle, unperturbed by her gibe. "I'm afraid that neither of us has made a very favorable impression on Mrs. Sprague. . . ."

That is not entirely true, she was compelled to admit to herself, trying hard not to let her gaze linger on the sensuous curve of his smile, or the interesting little cleft in his rugged chin. Her opinion of him had changed a bit since her initial reaction. After witnessing him handle his attacker with cool aplomb, despite his weakened state, she no longer thought of him as "bumbling." Not in the least. Furthermore, she reminded herself, he had organized their retreat and the logistics of abandoning the carriage with admirable efficiency—

"We shall have to see if we can't think of something to do in order to win her regard," he continued in a soft drawl. "A daunting challenge, to be sure, but one well worth the effort." Though the light was dim, Aurora could swear he had the nerve to wink.

To her chagrin, it was now her own cheeks that were taking on a decidedly warm color. *Drat the man.* Why was it, the simplest of his teasings seemed to set her to blushing like an untutored schoolgirl? It was most unlike her to let a man—*any* man—affect her composure. It was fortunate that he did not seem to expect a reply, for she was afraid that her voice would betray how easily he had penetrated her defenses.

But instead of continuing with another barrage of banter, Alex all at once became quite grave. He pulled another crate up to the table and gestured for her to take a seat. "However, in the meantime, perhaps you would consent to share your ideas with us. Heaven knows, we can use all the help we can get if we are to get to the bottom of this conundrum in time."

Aurora wasn't quite sure he was being serious. "You are really asking for my opinion?" she asked with some surprise.

He nodded. "You have certainly shown yourself to possess a sharp mind, and from what you told me at our first encounter, you appear to have a great deal of experience in the field of, shall we say, discreet investigation. We would be fools to ignore your opinion simply on account of your . . . plumbing, wouldn't we, Jack?"

The other man gave a strangled cough.

Aurora chose to accept the horrified wheeze as a "yes" and sat down. "Very well. Now, let me make sure I overheard you correctly—the crux of the dilemma centers on the fact that it seems impossible for any of the suspects to be a traitor. Correct?"

Both of them nodded.

"Well, then it is," she announced.

Jack, she noticed, was watching her with the same sort of glazed expression that a mouse might regard a snake. "Is what?" he asked faintly.

"If it *seems* impossible, then most likely it *is* impossible," she explained. "My guess would be that the real villain is not one of the gentlemen in question, but someone close to him. Someone to whom he might unwittingly reveal, if pressed skillfully enough in an unguarded moment, a good deal more than he should."

Alex laced his fingers behind his head and fixed her with a keen look. In the flickering shadows it was difficult to discern exactly what was lurking in the blue depths of his eyes, but his words seemed clear enough. "Bravo, my dear. And whom would *you* be looking for, Aurora?"

"A trusted friend, perhaps from one's schooldays. The sort of fellow one would share a bottle of port with at one's club," murmured Jack before she could answer. "Hmm, that is—"

The corners of Alex's mouth curled up just a bit. "A logical suggestion, but I don't think that's exactly whom she had in mind. And I believe the unguarded moment she is referring to is a bit more intimate than drinking spirits at White's."

"Precisely, sir," replied Aurora briskly, trying not to think about what a strange effect that suggestion of a smile, as well as the sound of her name on his lips, was having on her pulse. *Lord, since when had a man's offhand approval sent her insides into such a tizzy?* She cupped her chin in her hand, as if that might help her get a grip on her emotions, and spent some moments in thought. "To begin with," she finally said, "I would ask myself if any of these gentlemen has a wife or a mistress who might be suspect." Her lips then pursed for an instant. "On second thought, I would say it would definitely be a mistress. Men are much more apt to try to impress their ladybirds with their importance than their wives. . . ."

Both men stirred rather uncomfortably on their seats.

"And secondly, a woman who makes her living in . . . such a business must be practical and think of one day retiring. I would imagine the amount paid for the type of information that is being sold would free a woman from any financial worries for the rest of her life."

"A most interesting idea," murmured Jack, in obvious fascination.

"What sort of woman would we be looking for?" added Alex.

"One who is clever and resourceful. One who is practical enough to do meticulous planning and imaginative enough to be able to improvise if things go awry. And most of all, one who has the nerve and resolve to take great risks in order to get what she desires."

"Sounds very much like you." As Aurora's mouth fell open in indignant protest, he grinned. "Except for the, er, business part, of course."

"Hmmph!" Resisting the childish urge to stick out her tongue, she merely narrowed her eyes and gave him what she hoped was a piercing glare before turning away with an audible sniff. "As I was saying, sir," she went on, directing her words to Jack alone. "Is there anyone among your suspects who might be prone to be boastful? Or in need of being told how very clever he is?"

He scratched at his thatch of chestnut curls. "Now that you mention it, Dearbourne or Meechum might be possible candidates. Both think rather highly of themselves, and both have . . . expensive *cher amies.*"

His choice of a French phrase set Aurora to thinking. "*Cher amies*—I don't suppose either of the ladies in question has anything so obvious as a French parent?"

A look of dawning comprehension spread across Jack's face, followed by one of undisguised admiration. "By Jove, what a clever idea, Mrs. Sprague! I should never have thought of something like that." He spent some time mulling over the question. "It may be nothing important, but I think I remember some rumors about Dearbourne's, er, lady having spent some time in Paris."

"Would either of you recognize her on sight?"

Alex shook his head. "It has been some time since I was last in London. What about you, Jack?"

"Ah, I do believe I have seen her at the opera and, er, perhaps at several other places."

"Well, then, that is one face to be watching for." Aurora drummed her fingers on the rough wood of the table. "But don't expect her to make it easy for you. She'll not act or dress as she would in London. No, this woman has shown herself to be extremely clever. Be on the lookout for an aging lady's maid or a simple farmer's wife."

"You think she may be a master at disguise?" asked Jack with some incredulity.

Aurora permitted herself a slight smile. "Of course. Females in her line of work understand all too well the art of appearance." She then stood up and gave a small yawn. "Now, if you gentlemen have no further questions, I think I will lie down for a bit."

Jack scrambled to his feet, while Alex took a bit more time in rising. "I think I shall do the same," he announced. After a bit of a stretch he removed his jacket and started for the back room.

"A-are you going to—"

"Sleep with you?" He finished off the sentence when it became clear the words were stuck in her throat. "A lovely offer, but I'm afraid I'm too tired to be at my best. Another time, maybe."

"Conceited oaf," she muttered through clenched teeth, mortified that yet again he had managed to bring a burn to her cheeks.

Alex was already dragging the second pallet into the main room. "Just teasing, Aurora."

She was about to inform him that she had not granted him leave to use her given name with such irritating regularity when she saw a spasm of pain squeeze the laughter from his eyes. "Let Jack finish with that, sir. The bandage on your shoulder needs to be changed." The edge was gone from her voice, replaced by a stab of concern. "Sit down and let me attend to it."

He looked up, surprised. "You needn't trouble yourself. I've dealt with plenty of scratches over the years. If I need a hand, Jack can help with the dressing."

Such assurances caused the other man to go a bit pale. "Ah, actually, I'm not sure that I am—"

"Males usually make a hash of such things—that is, if they don't keel over first. Really, one would think that given your penchant for violence, you men wouldn't be so squeamish at the sight of a little blood." She disappeared for a moment, then returned with her reticule in hand. "I took the precaution of keeping a roll of clean linen in here."

"A shame that the flask of brandy wasn't as pliable as cloth," quipped Alex.

"Oh, it wasn't the spirits that shattered, it was the bottle of vinaigrette. So don't faint again."

"I didn't faint," he murmured. "But why on earth do you carry vinaigrette? Somehow I can't imagine you ever succumbing to a fit of girlish vapors."

"It makes sense to be prepared for every contingency." Her fingers peeled back the shirt from his shoulder. "Jack, I don't suppose you have a bowl that I might use for the water?"

The other man rummaged in his rucksack and managed to locate a battered tin cup.

"That will do." Aurora unwrapped the old bandage, then extracted another bit of cloth, along with a glass vial, from her reticule. After dampening the rag, she began to swab at the jagged wound. Jack made a strange sound in the back of his throat and offered to refill the jug. He was out the door without waiting for a reply.

"OUCH!"

"Stay still! That could not possibly have hurt."

Alex winced as she probed a different spot. "You are enjoying this, aren't you?"

"Immensely." Satisfied that there was no sign of infection, she sprinkled a liberal amount of basilicum over the raw flesh and started to wind the fresh linen in place. As she worked, her head came close to his and she could feel the soft whisper of his breath against the lobe of her ear. It stirred a lock of her hair, causing it to fall over the rise of her cheek. Her hand moved to brush it back, but his was quicker.

"Allow me." With a deft touch, he tucked it behind her ear, but his fingers lingered, toying with a strand or two of the errant curls. "You know, you are truly a female of admirable talents."

Aurora ducked her head. "Most any farm wife knows how to bind up a simple injury. Yours doesn't look to be of concern anymore. It seems you are well out of danger." She wished the same could be said for herself. Good Lord, the man's touch was sending a heat worse than any fever coursing through her veins, and all of a sudden it was getting rather difficult to breathe.

"Grateful as I am for your practical skills, it is your sharp mind and invaluable insight that I was referring to. I daresay if we succeed in stopping the traitor, it will be in no small part due to you."

The small room appeared to be tilting at an odd angle. Reaching out to steady herself, Aurora found her hand splayed across his bare chest. "I-I am happy if a few of my suggestions have proved useful."

Now, if only she had a suggestion for how to ignore the strange things his proximity was doing to her insides! All her strength had mysteriously melted away, leaving her limbs feeling like jelly. In another moment, she realized, she would plop into his lap, her quivering lips inches from his.

She closed her eyes tightly, trying to put out of her mind

the memory of that first kiss between them. *Hell's bells.* The
man had been half dead and still his embrace had left her
nearly senseless. Surely a fresh assault would render her—

"Er . . ." Jack paused at the door and shifted the jug to his
other hand. "Perhaps I should—"

"I've just finished with the M-ma—"

"Alex," he corrected.

"With Alex," she finished, hoping her face was not as
scarlet as a soldier's tunic as she scrambled out of her awkward position. "He seems to be recovering nicely."

Jack cleared his throat, making a noise that, to Aurora's
burning ears, sounded suspiciously like a strangled chuckle.
"Yes, so it appears."

"I swear," she whispered, taking a quick look at the
amusement bubbling up in Alex's eyes, "if you say one rude
comment—just one—the next bandage will be wrapped
around your throat!" Straightening her skirts, she stepped
over to the table and made a show of putting her supplies
back in her reticule.

Her attention, however, was not so engaged that she
didn't see him sway slightly as he stood up. A second glance
made it evident that beneath the stubble and dirt and grinning bravado, his face had become more pale than she
would have liked. "You had better lie down." Turning to
Jack, she added, "Do you think we might venture a fire a bit
later? He needs something hot to drink."

"I don't need any coddling," snapped Alex. "Just need an
hour or two of sleep."

Aurora ignored him. "Perhaps you might ride into the
nearest town and get the following. . . ." She rummaged
around in her bag for a pencil and a scrap of paper, then
scribbled a short list.

"I was planning on doing a bit of reconnoitering, ma'am,
so I'm sure I can find what you want."

"Stay away from the coast just yet," warned Alex. "Until

we have made further plans, we don't want to alert our quarry to our presence."

"Right. I thought I would head to Kilmarnock. It's on the main coaching road and with some discreet questions, it may be possible to learn a few things about the recent comings and goings. And since it is one of the larger towns in the area, I shall also be able to pick up some supplies and another horse there without attracting attention." He took up his rucksack. "Anything else you might need, ma'am?"

"No, not at the moment." She walked over and handed him her list. "Oh, you may as well call me Aurora, too, as it seems we are all going to get to know each other rather well over the next little while."

He grinned. "With pleasure, Aurora."

As her back was turned, she didn't see the color of the earl's eyes darken a shade, or the slight frown that tightened his lips as Jack said her name.

Chapter Six

Alex splashed a bit of water on his face and wiped away the worst of the grime with the tail of his shirt. Perhaps a fire was not a bad idea. With some hot water he might at least manage a decent shave. And though the river was rather chilly, a bath might be in order, too. Judging by the state of his dusty jacket and breeches, the rest of his person must be in none too pristine a state.

After a slight hesitation, he stripped off his clothes and slid into the rippling current. It was several hours past noon and the sun had burned off the morning clouds, dappling the tall grasses with a mellow warmth that looked even more inviting from where he was sitting. Ducking his head under the water, he threaded his fingers through his tangled locks, then grabbed up his garments and gave them a quick rinse as well. The years of rough camp life had made him well used to such primitive conditions. With practiced ease, he scrambled back up the bank, wrung out the mass of soaking cloth, and draped the items over a nearby bush to dry.

For his own dripping body he chose a patch of gently

swaying meadowlark and ryegrass. The sun's rays soon stilled the chattering of his teeth, and the sensation of the icy numbness ebbing away to a pleasant warmth left him quite content to linger until his clothes were dry as well.

As his eyes fell half closed, Alex couldn't help but think on how, after years of enduring the hardship and uncertainties of soldiering, his life was about to change dramatically. It was hard to imagine that this was to be his last mission. No more baths in cold rivers or weevilly biscuits for supper. The rough camaraderie of his fellow officers was about to be replaced by the polished small talk of the *ton*. A foray into enemy territory would soon mean attending one of the myriad glittering balls and facing the matchmaking mamas curious as to whether the new Earl of Woodbridge was . . . available.

An oath formed on his lips. *Hell's teeth*. He wasn't sure he didn't prefer the threats of actual warfare to those of Polite Society. The thought of standing up to mere physical danger was far less intimidating than the idea of living with subtle innuendo and whispered rumors. Never had he been accused of cowardice, but a part of him wanted to flee—to Spain, to India, to the ends of the earth. Anywhere where he might avoid facing the future. Or the past.

It was, however, inevitable. His sense of duty and honor would not let him desert his duties. He would return to London when this mission was finished and figure out how to deal with what the vagaries of life had placed in his hands. All the things he had never wanted—a title, a fortune, a vast estate. And a wife.

The thought of his unknown bride brought the chill back to his bones. Good Lord, he had never even seen her face! All he recalled was that she was very small and very young. Perhaps she had been as much a pawn in the game as he had been, but somehow he doubted it. The son of an earl, even a younger one, was a far greater catch than any daughter of a reprobate baron might hope to land. No doubt the little witch had been happy to go along with the travesty of a wedding, well satisfied at thinking she was soon to be mistress of her own estate, however small and run-down. His lips compressed. And now, she must be rubbing her hands with glee at learning she had become a countess in the bargain.

Alex gave vent to a harsh sigh. Yes, in his experience, all females—young or old, titled or not—looked to gain something from a man, be it profit, prestige, protection, or simple pleasure. There was no reason to think his nominal wife, the female who had robbed him of his freedom of choice, was any different from the rest of her sex.

Is any woman? he asked himself with a sardonic grimace. To his own bemused surprise, the answer to such jaded cynicism that slowly took form in his head was not quite what he expected.

Perhaps there was one.

Aurora Sprague. Now there was a singular young lady. One who was, inarguably, unlike any other female he had ever encountered. She was as brave and resourceful as any of his brother officers, which, Alex realized with a rueful smile, was about as high a praise as he could bestow on anyone. Rather than resorting to shrieks and tears when confronted with danger, she had displayed a feisty courage, relying on her own wits and determination to see her through.

Her outer toughness could not, however, hide what lay beneath the steely demeanor and guarded words. From the few facts he had gleaned concerning her current activities, it had become clear that she had undertaken an arduous—and expensive—journey in order to help a female of no relation, simply because the poor woman had no one else to turn to. She might claim that this rather bizarre hobby of hers was inspired simply by dislike of men, but he sensed it stemmed from far nobler sentiments. Though she seemed loath to admit it, even to herself, kindness and compassion lay at the core of her being rather than the cold cynicism she chose to wear as one would a suit of armor.

His expression became very pensive. Certainly she had revealed a softer side in caring for him. Softer and more vulnerable. It seemed she expected nothing in return. He admitted that it was beyond his experience. It was unexpected. As was just about everything about her.

Yet another quality that had earned his grudging admiration was how she was pluck to the bone. Why, not once since he had accosted her in the gloom of her carriage had she complained of being tired or hungry or uncomfortable. Or, for that matter, any of the myriad discomforts that would have driven another female into a state of permanent hysterics.

It was not that she lacked certain other feminine . . . attributes. *Very* feminine, he might add. Though her gown was hardly designed to flatter her figure, it revealed enough of the slim, rounded hips and firm, ripe swell of bosom to have his thoughts straying far from the mission at hand.

Good Lord, it was his own desires that were turning traitorous on him. Never before had he allowed anything— much less a woman—distract him from his duties. With a start, he realized that instead of concentrating on how to ensnare a dangerous spy, his attention had been focused on a very different sort of lady, and how he might capture . . .

Capture what? That gave him pause for thought. Oh, he wanted her. Strangely enough, more than he had ever wanted a woman before, though he could not quite explain why, even to himself. There was no question that she was not as beautiful as some of the women in his past. Nor did she lure him on with coy flirtations or seductive charm. A soft chuckle stole forth from his lips. *Ha!* Her idea of a murmured endearment had been a threat to strangle him.

An odd half smile played at the corners of his mouth,

then quickly faded as he reminded himself that all females were adversaries of a sort. The fact that Mrs. Sprague was married and no innocent made her fair game. He was free to pursue her as ruthlessly as he meant to go after the true enemy. After all, it was clear from a number of her comments that she knew the rules and expected no quarter from men.

Alex found himself staring at the scudding clouds, their shapes changing with quixotic whim from moment to moment. Suddenly, desire was tempered by a twinge of regret, even guilt. *That was the damn problem,* he realized. Though why it should bother him that the young lady had been hurt in the past eluded any reasonable explanation. The stirrings of a conscience—that is, if he had one when it came to his dealings with women—was an unfamiliar sensation, and one he sought to still just as quickly as it had arisen. It wasn't as if her life, however tragic, had aught to do with him. He had always been most careful to keep an emotional detachment from any female, especially those he had taken to his bed. This shouldn't be any different.

Damnation, he muttered again. He must still be suffering the effects of his fever to confuse simple lust with any other more complex feelings.

"Alex? Are you out there?" Aurora's voice, tight with concern, floated across the field. The cry sounded again, louder this time.

He sat upright. "Yes, I'm over here."

"Oh!" She turned and rushed forward in his direction. "I feared you might have . . . passed out again."

He started to rise, then quickly thought better of it. "Er, you had better stop where you are."

"B-but why?"

"Because if you take another step, you are going to see a great deal more of me than just my great hairy legs." He pointed to the bush where his clothes were hung. "If you would be so good as to turn around for a moment, I shall fetch my things."

She did as he requested, but not before he saw her eyes flare and her face turn a distinct shade of crimson. Good Lord, did she have any idea how utterly provocative she looked when she was in high color? With a mischievous grin, he couldn't resist adding, "And no peeking."

"Hmmph." She tossed her head. "As if I should find the view in that direction of any interest whatsoever."

A peal of laughter greeted the steely retort. "I am lucky your razor tongue is the only sharp implement you are wielding at the moment, else I should be forced to turn tail and run," he murmured, drawing another indignant snort. "Even so, it has dealt the most grievous of all the wounds I have suffered over the past few days." His fingers finished with the buttons of his breeches, then tugged on his shirt. "There. You may now admire the view with utmost propriety."

Aurora made a point of walking toward the river without so much as a glance in his direction. He hurried to catch up and fell in with her stride. "Forgive my teasing. I did not mean to set your back up, but it is hard to resist when you look so very becoming with a flash in your eyes and a glow on your cheeks."

To his surprise, a pinch of longing seemed to tug at her features before it was quickly brushed away by a look of wariness. "Surely you are not flirting with me, Major Woodmore?"

"Alex," he reminded her. "And why not? Most any man would find it impossible not to engage in a little harmless flirtation with a pretty lady." On catching a glimpse of the surprise that flickered for a moment in her eyes, he added, "Can it be that you are not used to men flirting with you, Aurora?"

She stumbled, nearly losing her balance on the rocky

ground. "You have spent too much time on the Peninsula, sir, for your compliments have the ring of Spanish coin." Shaking off the hand he had placed on her elbow, she stalked to the edge of the bank and peered down at the swirling water. "What I wouldn't give to wash away the dust and grime, too," she sighed, her words hardly more than a low whisper.

"You wish to bathe?" Alex came up behind her. "Then go ahead. I promise I shall be as steadfast as you were about not peeking. I warn you though, it's cold as a witch's ti—er, that is, it's quite icy, but there is a shallow pool just a little farther on. Here"—he peeled off his shirt—"you may use this to dry yourself. And if you leave your things on the bank, I'll give them a good scrubbing and hang them up to dry."

A look of utter disbelief spread across her face.

His eyes twinkled. "Army life teaches one a great deal of useful skills."

"More useful than those most men possess," she replied, but there was little sting to the words. After another look of longing at the water, she turned back to him. "You promise you will not . . . look?"

"Word of honor." Alex draped his shirt over her shoulder. "Hurry along, while the sun is still warm. I'll go back to the cottage as soon as I am done, so you may come out whenever you wish."

Flashing him a grateful smile, Aurora hurried toward the spot he had indicated.

After he hung up her wet garments, Alex forced his steps to continue away from the splash and gurgle of the river. His word was his word, he thought with wry resignation, and however strong the current of his desire, he had to abide by his pledge. But that didn't mean he couldn't try to imagine what usually lay beneath the folds of faded muslin. The graceful sway of her hips hinted at just the sort of rounded curves he longed to run his hands over and the swell of the breasts looked firm and ripe, their rosy buds ready to be taken between his teeth and teased to arousal.

Such thoughts brought back the memory of how those expressive lips of hers had felt pressed against his. Beneath the scowls and grimaces, they were tantalizingly soft and pliable. Lord, she was not nearly as cold or indifferent as she wished people to think. There was molten fire under the steel, he was sure. He had felt it in her initial response. Just as he had also felt her inexperience, her fear at intimacy.

His brows drew together in consternation. *What sort of fool was her husband, to ignore her charms?*

That was not his concern, Alex reminded himself none too gently as he threw the rough door of the cottage open and stepped into the gloom. Yet he found it hard to banish from his mind the fleeting look of need in the young lady's eyes, made more poignant by the fact that she tried so very hard to keep it hidden. At that very moment, had the cursed fellow been present, there might have been hell to pay.

"Has your shoulder taken a turn for the worse?" Jack looked up from sorting through the bag of supplies laid out on the table. Two battered iron pots lay on the floor, as did a small pile of kindling.

Alex growled something unintelligible, then took a seat on one of the crates. "Did you learn anything of interest?"

"I—" Jack paused and darted a look around the darkened interior. "Er, perhaps we should wait for Aurora to be present too, seeing as she seems to have some interesting ideas on the subject." There was an awkward cough. "I'll go fill the water jug for her while we wait—"

"You will *not!*" At the look of surprise that sprang to the other man's face, Alex made a grudging explanation. "She is taking a . . . bath."

The puzzled grimace tweaked into a rakish smile. "Lord, I am tempted to forget I am a gentleman and revert to the antics of a randy schoolboy, spying on the local village lasses."

"I gave her my word she would not be disturbed." The note of command in Alex's voice was unmistakable.

Jack fixed him with a speculative gaze. "I thought you said you had not engaged in any, er, intimacies with—"

"I did! I mean, I didn't!"

The other man's eyes took on a certain glitter. "She is quite a lovely young lady, and one free to indulge in a dalliance. If you have no claim, then I am tempted to see if she might be willing—"

"No!" Alex shifted uncomfortably on the wooden slats. "The devil take it, man," he growled. "What I mean is, since I dragged her into this affair, she is under my . . . protection until I can see her safely returned to her home. I take it my meaning is clear?" Even as he spoke, Alex couldn't help but wonder what had prompted such an outburst. It was hardly his right to object if Jack wished to attempt a seduction. Why, just a short time ago, he, too, had been thinking improper thoughts with regard to the young lady's person. But somehow, the idea of another man's eyes—or hands—roaming over that lovely body caused a clenching of his fists, and not simply because he wished to keep such pleasures reserved for himself. Confused by his own conflicting emotions, he muttered a sharp oath. "Come now, it's time we started thinking with our brains rather than our loins. Tell me what you have discovered."

The other man's brow furrowed slightly, but he made no reply other than to unfold a piece of paper and push it across the table. Alex took it up and skimmed over the scribbled notes. "So," he said after a few moments, "three possible suspects have passed through Kilmarnock."

Jack nodded.

"Hmm. We had better study what other route a traveler might take when coming from the south. . . ."

Soon the only sinuous curves that held thrall on their attention were the fine lines and squiggles on the rough map

Jack had retrieved from his rucksack. So busy were they studying the roads and terrain leading to the coast that neither heard the faint rasp of the iron hinges as the door pushed open.

Aurora stood at the threshold, the light filtering through the still-damp hair that cascaded down over one shoulder. Highlights of red and gold tangled around her fingers as they combed through the silky strands. "Do you wish for me to wait outside while you finish with your plottings?"

"You are—" Jack was already on his feet, but his words seemed to lag behind. Swallowing hard, he looked from her to Alex.

Alex stared at the play of sun and shadows upon her features, suddenly very aware of every subtle detail—the tilt of her chin, the plane of her cheekbones, the fullness of her mouth, and the vibrancy of her eyes. A faint prickling sensation stirred over his bare skin and he looked away. "You are, of course, welcome to listen in," he said gruffly, turning his attention back to the map. "The sooner we solve this, the better."

Aurora gave one last tug at her tresses before crossing the threshold. What a strange and quixotic man this stranger was, she mused, all leers and laughter one moment, coldly calculating the next. He was certainly unlike any gentleman of her acquaintance—not that there had been that many!

Her limited contact with the opposite sex had left her with the distinct impression that men were, in general, vain, shallow, self-centered, and prone by their very nature to be bullies. But while the major possessed a goodly amount of arrogance and was obviously used to having his word obeyed, she sensed there was a great deal more depth to his character than just that. It was difficult to put into words. There was an undeniable strength about him, yet oddly enough, it was more comforting than intimidating. He was kind as well, though he chose to mask it with casual bravado. Perhaps even odder was the fact that he appeared able to recognize his own foibles and find some measure of ironic humor from them.

Now, that was truly a rarity—a man who could laugh at himself.

"Your shirt is almost dry, sir." She draped it over his shoulders as she passed by, taking great care not to touch the tanned flesh. "Put it on before you catch cold. I should not wish to be accused of sabotaging the mission, all for want of a bath." Spying the pots on the earthen floor and the sack of provisions on the table, she scooped them up and made toward the small hearth. "Why don't I see to some supper while you go on with your plans."

A short while later the rich aroma of a simmering stew wafted up with the spreading warmth of the fire, causing the two men to pause for a moment in their measurements and calculations.

"By Jove, Mr. Sprague is a singularly lucky fellow," murmured Jack as Aurora stirred some of the fresh herbs she had gathered into the mixture of lamb and turnips. "I hope he recognizes his good fortune in having a wife who is beautiful, clever, and a marvelous cook, to judge by the smells drifting our way."

Aurora's knuckles went very white from the force with which she clenched the wooden spoon.

Unaware of her reaction, he continued on in the same light vein. "Why, if you were not already taken, I should consider falling on bended knee—"

"Such a romantic gesture would be entirely wasted on me. I don't plan to *ever* walk to the altar again." Her mouth set in a tight line. "Not that I chose to do so the first time."

All the humor went out of Jack's face. "Please forgive such cowhanded teasing. I-I did not mean to . . . upset you in any way," he finished lamely. Striving to understand the source of her agitation, he added, "Is your husband, however unlamented, recently deceased, then?"

There was an awkward silence before Aurora answered. "I have no idea," she said with exaggerated unconcern. "Nor do I care." Carefully ladling a generous helping from the pot into each of the tin bowls Jack had brought from town, she carried them to the table. "Are you married, Jack?" she asked abruptly.

He shook his head.

"Then it is *you* who are the fortunate one."

There was no reply, only a slight creasing of his brow as he bent his head and began to pick at his food.

"I'm afraid that like us, Jack, Aurora has taken on the sort of duties that have given her a rather jaded view of the human race. Men in particular." Alex had not yet touched his stew and Aurora was all too aware of how his gaze had remained focused on her face. "Actually, now that I have my wits about me, I am more than a little curious to hear in more detail about the working of Sprague Agency for Distressed Females."

Jack made a choking sound.

"That is," continued Alex, "if it wouldn't be too . . . distressing."

Striving to mask what those probing blue eyes were doing to her insides, she gave a careless shrug. "You've heard the gist of it. Women come to me with a problem, one that usually involves men. Using common sense and reliable sources I am almost always able to solve it."

"For example?" Jack's spoon hung in midair, stew untouched.

Aurora rubbed at her chin. "Let me see, there was a certain . . . lady of title whose husband was being particularly intransigent about untying the purse strings for a Season in Town. Claimed there wasn't enough blunt for it even though the lady in question had brought a hefty fortune as a dowry.

Now, she was sensible enough to decide the little matter was worth investigating, so she came to me."

"And then?" prompted Jack, who was clearly hanging on every word.

"And then only the good Lord could help the poor devil," quipped Alex with an amused chuckle.

Aurora ignored his interruption. "Well, it was really quite simple. The pompous prig was so sure of himself that he consigned his frequent billet-doux to the waste bin, where any maid might retrieve them, rather than locking them away in his desk or burning them in the grate. He also made the rather foolish mistake of riding past where the milk-maids churned the cream on his way to the summer house by the lake. That made it even easier to discover that he was tossing up the skirts of not one but three of the local ladies."

Both men made a weak attempt at a grin.

"Once I had the basic information in hand, it was child's play to make a quick trip into the nearest town of any note and visit the purveyors of such fripperies as filigree ear bobs, silk parasols, and the like, always implying how much I wished to emulate a certain gentleman's purchases. The list was quite extensive." There was nothing forced about the smile that spread over Aurora's lips. "When presented with a full overview of the situation, he became eminently rea-sonable about how expenses might be reallocated to allow his wife to spend time—and a full purse—in London."

Jack made a convulsive swallow, but not of any morsel of lamb or turnip. "Amazing. I, er, understand now how you have come by your expertise in the field."

"Of course," she added, unable to suppress a touch of smugness in her voice, "there are the cases where a mer-chant or supplier simply seeks to cheat one of my clients be-cause she is a female, but those are usually not so interesting, for they involve little more than patience and a skill for arithmetic."

It was not hard to read the look of admiration writ across Jack's open face. Alex's expression was much more difficult to decipher, especially as he had turned away to contemplate the fire, as if the flickering embers were of more interest than any of her words.

What did it matter what he thought? she asked herself. She had long ago left off caring what others thought of her.

Was it because rejection still had the power to wound after all these years?

Aurora shoved such disquieting insight aside, along her unfinished meal. As she made to rise, Jack ventured a tentative question. "I do not mean to pry, Aurora, but it is clear from your speech and your manners that you are a lady. . . ." His voice trailed off in question.

She ducked her head. "My father was a baronet."

"And Mr. Sprague?"

"A younger son."

"You did not care for the match?"

"I was not of an age to object."

Jack's brows drew together. "Sprague," he repeated. "From what part of the country did you say he—"

"I didn't. Please, I really do not wish to discuss the matter any further. It has absolutely nothing to do with our current situation. And seeing as in a few days we will go our separate ways and never see each other again, it is just as well to remain . . . strangers."

He nodded. "As you wish." Then, following her lead, quickly changed the subject. "Speaking of our mission, you have heard the information I managed to pick up in Kilmarnock. Is there anything you wish to add to our plans?"

She turned the question over in her mind. "Not as of yet, but I would counsel you to keep alert. I do not share in your belief that she will not show up because the major is here."

"And why is that?" Alex's eyes were half closed and his voice came in a lazy whisper.

"Because men are not the only ones for whom danger is a potent elixir." Seeing she had startled him into full wakefulness, she went on. "We all agree the spy you seek is both clever and willing to take great risks. My guess is that she sees herself as able to outwit you, regardless of the fact that you know she is coming."

It may have been a trick of the light, but Aurora thought she detected a glint of humor in his eyes.

"Well, then, may the best man win."

Chapter Seven

A gust of wind rattled the loose panes of glass in the tiny window above Aurora's head. The noise had not caused her to wake, for sleep had proven elusive, despite all that had happened. After a few more tosses and turns, she threw off the single blanket and reached for the shawl that had been folded at the bottom of her valise. Perhaps a breath of air would help dispel the strange mood that had gripped her since—since Alex had yanked her off her feet and into the carriage!

She had never quite regained her equilibrium. Usually nothing kept her off balance for long. No doubt it had something to do with the fact that she was not used to the presence of a man in her life. An overbearing man, she added, who thought he could order her around as if she were the rawest of recruits. An arrogant man, smugly sure of his irresistible appeal to the opposite sex, and one whose outrageous teasing and flirting made her feel—

Admit it! Aurora bit at her lip. Loath as she was to acknowledge the truth, there was no denying that his prac-

ticed charm, however hollow, made her feel . . . desirable.
And attractive. She had never really thought of herself in
such terms. After all, a female scorned by both her father
and her husband could hardly lay claim to an abundance of
either.

But Alex's casual words and searing kiss had kindled a
small spark somewhere deep within her, one that she dared
hope might someday, if properly fanned, ignite into a real
flame. *And pigs may fly!* she whispered aloud, mocking such
girlish dreams. Only a complete ninny would think that the
sort of romantic nonsense that warmed Robbie's heart took
form anywhere but on the printed page.

Pulling her shawl more tightly around her shoulders, she
rose from the thin pallet and crept noiselessly out into the
main room. A loud, rhythmic snoring greeted her entrance.
Good Lord, maybe the absence of a husband had its advantages, she mused as she tiptoed past a recumbent form. A
cough and gurgling sputter hurried her steps toward the
door. It was not latched and swung open at her touch with a
minimum of squeaking.

Clouds obscured all but the brightest stars and a damp-
ness in the air hinted at an approaching rain. Still, the cool
breeze felt good against her cheeks, chasing away the last
vestiges of her overheated imagination. Aurora stood very
still and tilted her head back, listening to the faint rushing of
water over the granite rocks, punctuated by the low hoot of
an owl.

"I would have thought you would welcome the opportunity for uninterrupted sleep."

She whirled around at the sound of the soft voice.

"What about you, sir?" she countered.

Alex stepped from the side of the cottage. "Perhaps a bit
later."

"You think it necessary to stand watch?"

"I think it prudent." He came to stand by her side, close

enough that she could breathe in the faint scent of bay rum, smoke, and peated malt, with an earthy undertone that was distinctly male.

Her fingers tugged at the corners of her wrap. "Now why is it that 'prudent' is hardly the adjective that comes to mind when I think of you, sir?"

In answer, a low chuckle rumbled somewhere deep in his throat. "Dare I inquire as to the other possibilities?" he asked. "Aside from 'bumbling,' 'odious,' and 'insufferable,' I may have missed a few of the other ones you muttered under your breath."

Not a one! Grateful that the darkness covered the embarrassed twist of her features, she searched for some appropriately pithy reply.

As if sensing her exact feelings, he chuckled again. "Don't worry. I've been called far worse things over the years." His hands clasped behind his back and his gaze strayed to the dark tangle of trees beyond the field. "And no doubt deserved them."

"Well, you are remarkably honest and forthright," she murmured. "Hardly adjectives that come to mind when speaking of men in general."

In the pale wash of moonlight, Aurora could see his lips twitch in amusement, then settle into a more pensive expression. "I suppose you have seen enough of our foibles to speak with some authority. Still, I'm sorry you have come to hold such a low opinion of us."

"It's hardly your fault," she murmured.

"It's my fault that you were dragged into this dangerous affair. By now you could be safely home with your Robbie rather than stuck here in the wilds with a total stranger—two total strangers."

A shiver ran down her spine. Somehow the prospect of home seemed rather more empty than it did several days ago. Before she could make a reply, his jacket came around her shoulders. "Sir!" she protested. "You've sacrificed quite enough of your garments for my comfort today."

"But not nearly enough for mine." His eyes were twinkling just like the stars. "That is, not counting the brief interlude after my bath."

"You are incorrigible, sir! Do you flirt so shamelessly with anybody who wears a skirt?"

He took a moment to stare up at the heavens. "No."

It was not the answer she'd expected. The teasing tone was gone, replaced by a deeper note that rung of melancholy or perhaps regret. Her head started to jerk around, only to find itself drawn down against his shoulder. She could feel the heat of him through the rumpled linen, and hear the steady beat of his heart. A good deal more steady than her own at the moment. Such intimate contact should have drawn a sharp rebuke, but for some reason, the protest died on her lips and she made no attempt to pull away.

"Do you see Orion?" he asked abruptly, pointing up at the stars. "According to Greek mythology, he was a hunter, pursued by the goddess Diana. When she accidentally killed him, she begged the gods to immortalize him in the night sky." He paused. "If you follow the line of his belt, it leads you to the North Star. There. Do you see it?"

She nodded.

"No matter where you are in the world, you can always find your way by using the constellations."

"A sad story." She shifted so that her cheek rested against the base of his neck. "What is it that you are hunting, Alex? And are you often lost?"

There was a flash of vulnerability in his eyes. "More times than I care to admit."

Aurora watched as the clouds scudded across the night sky, changing the pattern of winking lights with every passing second. "It is not always easy to discern the right path." The crescent moon was visible for an instant, only to disappear just as quickly. "The life of a soldier must not be an easy one. Why, many times, the choice is not yours to make."

The wry smile was back on his lips. "Perhaps that makes it the easiest life of all." His hand sought hers, enveloping it in his warmth. "And what of you, Aurora Sprague? Do you march along with steadfast steps, undaunted by any obstacle that may arise in your path, until you have arrived at your chosen destination?"

She wasn't sure how long they stood there in conversation. Like the clouds above, each of them revealed only random glimpses of their past lives. The words were cautious, guarded, intent on keeping many things well hidden, but by the time the first raindrop fell, they were no longer mere strangers.

"You had best go in, before you take a chill," murmured Alex.

That was quite unlikely, she thought, not with the warmth of his hand on hers, and the heat emanating from his chest. She found she was reluctant to give them up, but the wind kicked up and the drops began to fall with greater regularity.

"You must take shelter, too."

He walked her to the threshold. "I will, in a minute." His fingers slipped away. "Good night, Aurora."

"Good night, Alex." There was a moment of hesitation before she blurted out, "Nice."

His face betrayed his confusion. "What?"

"You asked me what other adjectives come to mind regarding you. 'Nice' is one."

As are "thoughtful," "perceptive," "wise," and "humorous," though she refrained from saying them aloud. The list could have stretched on quite a bit longer, for during their rambling conversation he had revealed more of himself than he might have guessed. Perhaps most surprising was the fact that he saw his own flaws and, indeed, could laugh at them.

In her experience, precious few people—especially men—possessed the strength to admit to weakness.

"You are a nice man, Alex Woodmore. And quite admirable, really. It seems that at heart you are a good deal less cynical than you would have people believe—including yourself." Without waiting for a response, she ducked her head and hurried inside.

Alex watched her disappear into the shadows. *Nice,* he repeated to himself. A number of ladies had paid him far more gilded compliments, but he didn't think any of the glittering phrases had affected him nearly as much as that simple word. He leaned back against the cold stone, keenly aware that a twist of her silky curls no longer tickled the underside of his chin. The emptiness there left him feeling . . . bereft. Lord, she had fitted into the crook of his arm like the missing piece of a puzzle.

And what adjectives might he choose to describe her? His fingers came up to rub along the line of his jaw. Mere words seemed inadequate to describe the whole of her. With a harried sigh, he realized that, if pressed, the first might have to be "bewitching"—too damn bewitching for his own peace of mind! From there, the list could go on to fill a ream of foolscap.

But "compassionate," "intelligent," "generous," "loyal" and "kind" were also among those that immediately sprang to mind. Some careful questioning had managed to coax from her a few more details about the so-called Sprague Agency for Distressed Females. Alex found himself shifting rather uncomfortably against the damp wall. He had never stopped to consider the differences between men and women except in terms of mere physical attributes. Her halting tales had opened his eyes, both to the hardships and injustices suffered by many females and to the deeper, more complex facets of her own character.

The clues were scattered at random throughout her conversation, but he was skilled enough at deduction to have guessed at the truth, or at least part of it. He was sure that despite her show of toughness, she had been deeply wounded by the men in her life. An unfeeling father, a hopeless husband. Rejection—even by those who deserved no regard—hurt, as he knew all too well.

Most people used their own private pain as an excuse to retreat, to give up on life. Aurora Sprague had used it as a challenge. She had refused to knuckle under, not to despair, not to the strictures of Society. She had fought back with rare courage, and each of her small victories had helped validate the struggle as well as to relieve the suffering of another. And through it all, she had not become dried and bitter, but had maintained vitality and a sense of humor.

Alex had met a number of extraordinary men through the course of his soldiering, but he didn't think he admired any of them more than he did the young lady who had fallen, quite literally, into his lap.

A glimmer of a smile flashed at the memory. Then his eyes pressed closed and lightness gave way to darkness. Would that he might remain blind to what else she had forced him to see! While the mirror of Aurora's words had revealed a good deal about herself, they had also made him take a close look at the full reflection of his own character. It was not an image of which he was proud.

As a soldier and a gentleman he could hold his head high. By anyone's standards, including his own, he had not lacked for honor, integrity, or courage in how he had comported himself. *But as a husband?* In that regard he had exhibited naught but cowardice and dereliction of duty, shirking all responsibility for his actions. The brutal truth of it was, Aurora had made him see he was little better than any of the other louts who so casually inflicted pain because Society said they had the legal and moral right to do so. Oh, his own cruelty had, of course, been more subtle than anything physical, but no less reprehensible. Why, in all the years since that fateful ceremony, he had hardly given more than a passing thought to the person who bore his name. His only concern had been for his own wants and needs. Never for a moment had he paused to wonder what her hopes, her dreams, her fears might be.

His jaw tightened. Under military law, he deserved to be shot. The real world, however, was a good deal more lenient to men of title and privilege. No, the only one who would judge his transgressions harshly was himself, and the only punishment he would suffer was the shame of knowing that he deserved Aurora's scorn rather than her admiration.

Somehow, he doubted "nice" would be the adjective that came to mind if she knew the truth.

He stepped out from under the thatched eaves and held his face up to the driving rain, wishing it could wash his conscience clean. It was some time before he went back inside the cottage, dripping wet and chilled to the very marrow.

The two men rode out just after first light, one heading north toward Ayr, the other turning south in the direction of Girvan. Aurora had shaken out the rolls of bedding, washed the tin bowls, and swept the earthen floor. Twice. She poked her head out the door and glowered at the leaden skies. It hardly looked promising weather for a walk, and in any case, she had been asked not to stray from the cottage, to avoid attracting any notice from the occasional passing shepherd.

Actually, that was not entirely correct—Jack had asked her, while Alex had simply barked a curt command to stay put.

Hmmph! As if it had been necessary to add the last little bit about trying not to get into any mischief that might jeopardize the mission! The nerve of the insufferable man! *She* had not been the one to accost the wrong suspect, or swoon so that they had to put up at an inn where one of the enemy might find them. With another sniff of indignation, she banged the door shut and stalked across the room to fetch her reticule. Perhaps she might find a piece of embroidery or clutch of knitting buried in its depths, she thought rather acidly, so that she might be seen to be engaged in a proper feminine pursuit when he returned!

And pigs might fly!

It was as if the words and the warmth that had passed between them last night had been no more than a fleeting dream. Alex had been brusque over tea and toast, his eyes studiously avoiding any contact with hers. There had been no invitation to participate in the brief strategy session, only a series of terse orders that had sent Jack scurrying for the door.

Had he regretted revealing that a soldier was not all steel, grit, and a blaze of scarlet and polished brass? Did he think that his humanity made him somehow   too vulnerable? Or perhaps on further reflection, he had simply taken a disgust of her and her radical ideas and actions. No doubt, if he were to choose an ideal female, she would be obedient, sweet-tempered, and enchantingly incapable of lifting a finger to do anything save summoning her maid.

Men! If all of them were so blasted quixotic in their moods, perhaps she was better off without one.

Her own mood turning even more sour, Aurora sat down at the table and began to pick out the shards of broken glass from her reticule. The tedious task was nearly done when her fingers brushed up against the spine of a book. She fished it out and regarded the gilt-stamped title. It was not one of her own choices, so Robbie must have taken it into her head to add one of those horrid novels she so favored to the bag. Well, it promised to be a long day, so she might as well take a peek.

Several hours later, as the last page was turned, Aurora shifted to ease the crick in her neck. Well, that wasn't quite as silly as she had imagined, even though the heroine was a bit too flighty for her taste and the hero lacked a dash of . . . A dash of what? She looked up from the book and propped her hand in her chin, giving the question her full attention. The gentleman in the story had no more depth to him than the paper of a printed page, she decided. He was so flat and one-dimensional that she imagined in the space of a short time, his charm would wear rather thin.

No, the sort of man able to bring the heat to her cheeks would need a good deal more substance to him. More mystery, more complexity, more . . . surprises. She paused as a small voice in the back of her head added that a shock of raven hair and sparkling sapphire eyes would not be amiss, either.

The cover of the novel closed with a decided snap. The notion that Alex Woodmore might cause any warmth to stir within her was only because the thought of him was, at the moment, making her blood boil. Oh, there was no denying that he was sinfully attractive, and that his kiss had ignited all sorts of strange sparks inside her that refused to die out. But he was also arrogant, overbearing, and altogether infuriating, she reminded herself. Hardly the stuff of storybook heroes.

Fingering the cording of the slim leather spine, she heaved a sigh and glanced around the room. It would still be some time before the two men could be expected home so she supposed there was nothing to do but fetch some other reading material from her valise.

Then her eyes fell on the battered canvas sack in the corner. Earlier in the morning, as she had straightened up Alex's things, she had noticed the corner of a book sticking out from among his belongings. She couldn't help but be curious about what sort of writings he would favor. Homer?

Virgil? The poetry of Wordsworth? Surely he wouldn't mind if she took a quick peek. Of course, it might only turn out to be some dry treatise on military theory, but anything would help to relieve the tedium of confinement.

The binding was frayed, the faded cloth dusty and faintly discolored with spatters of rain and salt spray. There was no printing of any kind on the front or the spine. It wasn't until she opened to the first page that the title appeared, the letters large and bold in a strange, sinuous typeface. *The Kama Sutra.* Underneath, in smaller print was written, *A Manual on the Divine Mysteries of Love from the Continent of India.*

Aurora had to repress a grin. So the sardonic major was really a romantic at heart, seeking to understand that most ethereal of human emotions. Her brow furrowed slightly at the subtitle. She had heard something of the French manuals on courtly love and chivalry written during the Middle Ages, but India . . . With a shrug, she flipped to the first chapter.

Oh dear.

That sort of love.

She blinked and turned the page. Then another.

Her cheeks were becoming very warm indeed. At one point she was forced to pause and turn the page upside down. Good Lord, if that was what went on in India, no wonder her husband had never come back!

The women she had worked with had never been shy about discussing the more graphic aspects of married life, especially as Aurora was supposedly an experienced woman herself. But their descriptions seemed rather . . . different from what was depicted in the detailed woodcuts. Looking a bit closer, she finally noticed there was some sort of text running along the bottom of the pages. Making herself a bit more comfortable on the hard crate, she began to read.

Chapter Eight

•

Aurora was so engrossed in the book that she failed to hear the faint creak of the hinges.

"Ah, how gratifying to see that you have actually obeyed my request to keep out of mischief."

Her head jerked up.

Alex stepped closer to the table and set down a small package of supplies wrapped in oilskin. His boots were spattered with mud, his jacket beaded with a light mizzle of drops, and his face lined with the fatigue of hours in the saddle. Still, a faint smile had come to his lips at the sight of her lovely neck arched in such studious concentration over the open pages. "Let me guess—the latest treatise from Mary Wollstonecraft?" he joked, making an effort to glance at the pages.

She tried to bury the volume in the folds of her skirts as two distinct spots of color rose to her cheeks. "N-no! That is, it is none of your business, sir, what sort of things I choose to r-read."

His brows drew together, first at the sharp edge of her

tone, then at the sight of a corner of the book's weather-beaten cover protruding from the dark muslin. It looked familiar. *Too familiar.* He reached for it, nearly causing Aurora to fall off the crate in an attempt to elude his hand. It was clear, however, that he did not mean to be denied, and aside from trying to squirm away in a most undignified manner, she was left with no choice but to surrender the item in her possession.

Alex took his time in regarding the pages she had been studying, his expression of bemused puzzlement slowly heating into one of scalding anger. It was not just the discovery of the racy book among his belongings that had his cheeks taking on the same guilty hue as Aurora's. There was a reasonable explanation for its presence among his belongings. Hidden among the graphic pictures was a set of coded ciphers, used to communicate with other clandestine agents. The trick had proved useful on more than one occasion, for an enemy searching his things had been far too distracted to recognize its real significance.

The real source of his embarrassment lay in wondering what else she had seen while rummaging through his bag. A muscle twitched, despite the clench of his jaw. There were copies of several recent letters between himself and his man of affairs that discussed his nominal wife and the terms of her quarterly allowance. Everything about them—their tone, the actual facts—would cast a less than favorable light upon him. Indeed, given her own rather strong sentiments on the subject, she would think him the worst sort of cad if she had read them.

Hell's teeth! A wave of self-loathing washed over him, followed by one of righteous anger. However unwittingly, she had scraped up against a wound that was, after all these years, still raw and festering beneath the scab. It hurt even more to think it might have been exposed to her, of all people. In retaliation, he parried with a thrust at what he knew was her own vulnerable spot.

"Indian fare is rather spicy, even for a married lady." His words were edged with a sardonic drawl. "Or perhaps your tastes run to the exotic. After all, you gallivant across the length and breadth of the land on your own, flouting every dictate of propriety while undertaking your outrageous endeavors, so it seems likely you crave the sort of excitement most gently bred females would never dream of. Was that why your husband left you, because of such ungovernable behavior?" He thumbed through several more drawings before adding roughly, "But it's nothing to worry on. I should be happy to take his place if you see anything that particularly whets your appetite."

Alex instantly regretted his crude comment as he watched her face go very pale, then color to a scarlet nearly as bright as the peppers used in a Madras curry. She turned away, but not quickly enough to hide the wounded look in her eyes. Well skilled in the art of attack, he had known just where to strike with greatest effect.

"I suppose I deserve to be the object of such scathing words, sir." Aurora drew in a deep breath, trying to steady the tremor in her voice. "But you may be assured, I need none of your mocking insults to remind me I lack the sweet manners, as well as the physical charms, of a normal female." Her hands twined into a knot in her lap. "I seem to engender a disgust in every man I meet, so your scorn hardly comes as a surprise."

Muttering something under his breath, he reached out and took hold of her chin, turning her around to face him despite her struggle to push away his hand. "I'm sorry," he said softly. "I didn't mean to say such despicable things. It was the shock of seeing my belongings had been searched—"

"I d-didn't look through the rest of your things, truly I did not! I saw the corner of the book sticking out from your bag

and did not think you would mind if I borrowed it for a bit."
She bit at her lower lip. "I-I thought it might be poetry, or at
least a treatise on battlefield tactics."

Alex gave a harried smile as relief and remorse surged
through him in equal measure. "Some might consider the relationship between men and women to be something akin to
war," he said with a wry grimace. "But I'll have you know,
the real reason this book is in my possession is that it hides
a set of military codes." There was a slight pause as he drew
in a breath. "I do not wish to be at daggers drawn with you,
Aurora. I hope that you will forgive my cutting words." His
grip softened to where it was almost a caress. "You remember that we agreed to avoid any personal questions? Well,
there are things in my bag that I would prefer remain . . . private."

"You have a right to be furious with me, sir. I had no
business touching your things."

"I'm not angry," he replied. His hand was still resting
against her skin and he was strangely reluctant to pull it
away. "Not with you." Her eyes flickered in question at his
enigmatic meaning, but instead of making any explanation,
he gave voice to his own query. "You really think you lack
any attraction for the opposite sex, Aurora?"

She wrenched away from his touch. "You needn't keep
teasing me, sir. I look in the mirror every day, and I don't
need a pair of spectacles to see quite clearly what stares
back."

"And what is it you think you see?"

"The same reflection as meets your gaze," she replied.
"That of a female well over the first bloom of youth, with
only passable features and hair a drab color, neither blond
nor auburn."

Alex wished he might do something—anything—to wipe
the look of haunting vulnerability from those features. Most
of all, he wanted to stop the slight tremor of her expressive

lips by covering them with his own and kissing her thoroughly. So thoroughly that she would cease to think the only reaction she inspired in a man was disgust. However, given what he had just said, she might misinterpret such an action. Besides, he reluctantly reminded himself, he had promised not to attempt another embrace without her consent, and despite his execrable conduct so far, he was determined to retain some shred of gentlemanly honor.

So instead, he decided he must be content with simply taking up a ringlet of her curls and gently rolling the silky strands between his thumb and forefinger. "Good Lord." He sighed. "I believe I shall have to order up a pair of special lenses if that is truly the image you see." There was a slight pause. "Blond would be insipid and auburn too garish. Your hair has a subtle complexity that is infinitely more intriguing. It is quite unique—like the rest of you."

Aurora blinked, too startled to react with anything more than a stare of disbelief. It took a few long moments before she finally regained some mastery over her emotions. "Back to your usual bald flirtations, I see." She leaned back slowly, disengaging her hair from his grasp. "You are a strange man, Alex Woodmore. One moment you are like one of your military sabers, all honed steel and sharp edges, hacking a swath through whatever stands in your way. Then the next you are . . ." Her voice faltered.

"Are what?" he demanded softly, wishing that he might slice off his own tongue for having brought such a look of hurt to her eyes.

"You are . . ."

The sound of hurried steps approaching the cottage caused her voice to cut off again. "Oh, it doesn't matter," she whispered as Jack threw open the door and made for the table, his eyes alight with unconcealed excitement.

"The deuce take it, Aurora, you were right!" he announced. "She was cunningly disguised, but I recognized

the profile. It's Dearbourne's ladybird. And she's with a man
who fits the description of your nocturnal visitor, Alex." He
consulted a pocket watch he had drawn from the pocket of
his coat as he spoke. "No vessel will be able to venture close
to shore until the tide turns, and that won't be until after ten
o'clock tonight." Looking up, he finally paused long enough
in his eager explanations to sense the tension in the small
room. "Er, is there something amiss?"

"Not at all," answered Alex through gritted teeth. "We
were merely discussing my own . . . unsatisfactory efforts of
the day." Restraining the urge to vent his frustration at the
untimely interruption by taking hold of Jack and tossing him
back out the door, Alex forced his mind to attend to what the
other man was saying rather than to dwell on the words that
might have come from Aurora's lips. He satisfied himself
with kicking one of the crates a little harder than necessary
in order to position it closer to the table. "It seems you have
had a good deal more success than I in discovering something of importance. Now, we had better get to work in re-
fining our plan of attack. . . ."

He dared only an occasional sideways glance at Aurora
as he and Jack began to discuss the details of their strategy.
It took all of his considerable control to maintain a facade of
rigid concentration, but in truth, half his mind was engaged
in wondering what emotions were hidden beneath her lowered lashes rather than what perils lay ahead in coming
hours. *Sweet Jesus,* he railed, hurling one curse after another
upon his mutinous thoughts. He was a seasoned soldier, not
some moonfaced halfling! How could he let his attention
wander from his duty?

Clenching his jaw so hard that his teeth threatened to
crack, he shifted in his seat so as to avoid all view of her
shadowed face. That helped somewhat and he finally managed to marshal his senses into some semblance of order.

An hour passed, maybe more. The two men spread out

several sheets of paper and eventually covered them with a number of scribbled diagrams as they debated the best way to construct a trap for the spy and her accomplice. Aurora made a terse response to the occasional question tossed her way, but other than that, she made no effort to join in. Withdrawing deeper into the slanting shadows, she set about coaxing the coals in the hearth to life, then put some water on to boil. The rest of the vegetables and mutton were added to the remnants of last night's meal, along with the last of the herbs, and the pot was hung above the flickering flames.

"I imagine you could use a bit of sustenance before you leave," she murmured, setting a bowl of the steaming stew in front of each man. Clearing her throat, she added, "Perhaps I might be of some use if I came along and—"

"No!" Alex's voice came out harsher than he intended. "You would only be a . . . distraction," he added haltingly. As soon as the words were out of his mouth, he realized how they only compounded the coldness of his initial exclamation. Lord, perhaps she was right, he thought with an inward grimace. Perhaps he *was* the most bumbling agent in all of Christendom, for at the moment he was certainly doing nothing to gainsay such a low opinion of his adroitness in dealing with any matter of a sensitive nature.

Aurora had turned a shade paler at his response, but made no argument. Jack merely arched his brows in vague reproach.

Drawing in a deep breath, he sought to salvage something of the situation. "You have been put in quite enough danger already," he growled. "I cannot in good conscience allow you to take any additional risk. You will remain here."

Her eyes refused to meet his. "Whatever you say. After all, you are the one in command, Major."

Why was it that her refusal to fight back left such a bitter taste in his mouth? He had become so accustomed to her feisty spirit and to the spark that flared in her eyes when she was ready to do battle, that this quiet surrender left him feeling more like a bullying lout than an officer deserving of respect.

Jack cleared his throat and sought to blunt the edge of sharp order. "Alex is right, Aurora. Your contribution has already proved invaluable, and to put you at physical risk would be unconscionable."

Alex gave an inward wince at the choice of words.

"Besides, I assure you that despite your initial impression, Alex and I are not quite so bumbling as you might have thought," he continued with a forced grin. "I promise we will manage not to make a mull of things on our own."

She didn't look up from tending the dying fire. "Of course."

Leaving his meal untouched, Alex rose abruptly and retreated to the corner of the room where his bag lay. He put away the book that he had kept carefully hidden away in his coat, then withdrew several other items. A slender sheathed knife went into his boot while the extra pistol was tucked in one of his pockets after the priming and flint had been checked.

A strained silence had descended over the room, save for the crackle of the burning kindling and the scrape of Jack's spoon against his bowl. Grimly aware of how badly he had handled things since his return to the cottage, Alex began to pace before the meager fire, wondering with each step how he had come to lose his bearings in such a precipitous fashion. Come to think of it, he realized with a start, he hadn't been able to hold a steady course since that fateful day when he had learned he was no longer Major Fenimore but the new Earl of Woodbridge.

Such disquieting thoughts were interrupted by Jack, who finally spoke up after making a show of consulting his timepiece. "I had best be off, as we planned."

Alex gave a curt nod. "I will follow shortly. You know where we are to meet up."

"Aye."

"Godspeed, Jack," called Aurora softly. "I wish you . . . well."

He shuffled his feet in some embarrassment. "The same to you, Aurora, though of course we shall be seeing each other shortly."

"Of course," she murmured. "Still, have a care."

"I will." Slanting a quick glance at Alex, he hurried to add, "Er, may I say now, it has been quite an experience working with a female such as yourself."

She smiled. "And one I doubt you care to repeat." The wry note of humor was unmistakable. "But you may breathe easy. I daresay you won't have to encounter many others like me."

"More's the pity," he said under his breath before slipping out the door.

Alex listened to the footsteps fading away into the gathering mist, feeling even more unsure of his own direction. His brooding gaze strayed from the dying flames to the swept hearth to the neatly arranged blankets—anywhere but to the young lady still seated in the shadows.

Suddenly he pivoted on his heel and made for the door.

"Alex—"

"Aurora—"

They both spoke at once.

She had risen, with a movement just as jerky as his, but before she could say another word he covered the space between them in three quick strides and was at her side. "Before you begin to ring a well-deserved peal over my head, let me apologize for my unforgivable conduct. Once again, you've seen a side of me that I am hardly proud of, but I"— his lips compressed in a tight line—"I can offer no excuse."

Her eyes dropped to the ground. "None is necessary.

There must be something about me that brings out the worst in men," she said in a small voice. As if realizing that the tone seemed to verge on self-pity, she immediately forced her mouth to quirk up and added, "No doubt a temperament befitting a mule and tongue more suited to a shrew have something to do with it."

Alex uttered a low oath, then tilted her chin up so that he could study every nuance of her mobile features. "Only a fool would fail to see the heart and courage of a lion." A harried sigh accompanied his whisper. "If, for some reason, things go . . . badly tonight, there is an extra purse sewn in at the bottom of my bag." He essayed a grim smile. "Do not hesitate to retrieve it and take yourself off to safety."

"Oh, Alex, promise me you will be careful!"

His expression was searching, though his words appeared to make light of the matter. "I would have thought you wouldn't mind in the least if someone put a bullet in my heart."

"N-no! That is . . ." A ragged intake of breath ended with an odd little sniffle.

It was with some shock that Alex realized that the watery catch in her voice was caused by a tear. His own throat tightened. *The devil take it!* To his memory, no one had ever really cared what became of him, much less cried over the thought that some harm might befall his person. Touched in a way he could not begin to explain, he pulled her gently toward his chest. Her chin was still cupped in his hand, and it took all of his wavering resolve to keep from using his lips to blot the salty drops from the arch of her cheekbone.

"Come now, sweeting. I shall reserve the right of putting the period to my existence just for you. Lord knows, you have first claim to it." His head was bent as he spoke, so that the warmth of her breathing tickled his skin.

With a movement so quick that it took him an instant to

be sure he hadn't imagined it, she rose on her toes and feathered her lips against his.

The kiss—if kiss was what it had been—left him not merely shocked but stunned. He tried to swallow, but somehow a lump had formed that was impossible to dislodge. Good Lord, was he really about to turn into a veritable watering pot himself? Such a lowering thought helped him choke down his emotions enough so that he could reply with dry humor. "I seem to recall a certain statement concerning flying pigs," he said with a rather crooked grin. "Am I hallucinating, or do I truly see swine soaring on gossamer wings?"

Aurora thumped a fist against his chest. "Wretch," she murmured. "Please don't remind me of such impetuous words. I-I sometimes say things I don't mean when I am angry."

"Don't we all?" He put his arms around her, drawing her so close he could feel the thud of her heart through the thick wool of his jacket. "Do you think that perhaps the porcine creatures might stay airborne long enough for you to grant me one more embrace? For luck."

This time it was more than a momentary brush. She lifted her head and the sweet curves of her lips, softly pliant and willing, molded to his. The taste of her was a subtle, shifting warmth, like early morning light. Thirsting for more, his tongue delved deeper, and when her mouth offered sustenance, he plunged into its depth with the desperation of a man finally escaping from years of drought.

She was more intoxicating than aged brandy, more potent than malt whiskey. With a low groan, he sought to drink his fill of her liquid fire. The heat was flooding every fiber of his being, from the tips of his fingers entwined in her curls to the throb of his groin pressed hard up against the softness of her middle. Her molten cry of his name nearly caused his

knees to buckle. Why, in another instant, he would be drunk
to all reason—

It was Aurora who helped to sober his spinning head.
Stumbling back a step from his embrace, she drew a ragged
breath and whispered, "I-I think you had better be going. It
wouldn't do to be late for your rendezvous with Jack."

A glib rejoinder floated toward his lips, but at the sight of
what was swirling in the depths of her emerald eyes, it stuck
in his throat. In answer, he pressed a gentle kiss to her forehead. "Yes," he sighed. "Duty must come before . . . all else."

"When duty is done, come back to me, Alex Woodmore."

"Of that you may be sure, sweeting. Haven't you learned
yet that I am a deuced difficult fellow to get rid of?"

The echo of his horse's pounding hooves had long since
died away, yet the thumping in Aurora's chest was still like
thunder in her ears. She ran her tongue over her swollen lips,
only to find that the taste of him lingered as well. Like a liberal shot of spirits, it was doing strange things to her equilibrium. Her legs seemed to be tilting at a most peculiar cant
while her stomach was engaged in a series of odd somer-
saults that left her breathless and a little dizzy. Taking her
head between her hands, she sunk down onto one of the
crates and tried to make some sense of what had just happened.

Surely her innate common sense, advanced years, and
previous experiences with the predatory nature of the opposite sex should have combined to make her immune to any
amorous advances from a gentleman. Yet here she was, in
danger of falling into a swoon at a mere kiss. One would
think she was an innocent schoolgirl, who had never been
kissed before!

She had, of course. Twice to be exact, counting this one.
Her lips gave a wry quirk. No matter that she hadn't ex-

perienced the sensation with great regularity, she still should
not be feeling as if her limbs had been turned to blancmange
nor should her insides be sliding around as if they were jel-
lied aspic on a platter. And above all, she most certainly
should not be wishing that Alex had made a complete meal
of her.

But she was. With a tiny gulp, she realized she had
wanted nothing so much as for his mouth to have continued
its ravenous plundering, his hands to have shredded her willing body into a thousand little morsels, to be consumed one
by one. He had made her feel delicious. Was it any wonder
that she had wanted to be devoured?

Silly goose!

Adding a rather more descriptive phrase she had overheard the coachman mutter, Aurora righted herself and
began to pace before the dying embers. All men had strong
appetites. Hadn't her investigations revealed that time and
again? So she must not be so bird-witted as to think that
Alex's hunger had been for her in particular.

But that did not account for her own sudden cravings.
She had never before felt that anything was missing from
her comfortable existence. Her little household—Robbie,
Alice, even Homer, the calico cat—had provided companionship, while her hobby had kept her wits exercised and her
days from becoming too flat. What more was there to wish
for in life?

Alex Woodmore, she answered with a sigh and a scrunch
of her mouth.

Oh, at times he could be as annoying as most men, showing the usual male penchant for overbearing arrogance and
petty tyranny. But such glaring flaws paled in light of his
other qualities. He had also shown himself to be kind,
strong, clever, and—wonder of wonders—willing to listen
to another opinion, even that of a female. No matter that
their exchanges sometimes involved a few thrusts and par-

ries. She enjoyed crossing verbal swords with him, for he had a honed intelligence and a sharp sense of humor.

Add to all that the fact that his piercing sapphire eyes and lithe, muscular form caused her insides to spark and quiver in a reaction that no aging female companion or furry feline creature seemed to elicit.

She paused in her pacing and stared at the narrow gold band on one of her left fingers. Worn to avoid tiresome explanations or prying queries, it now raised some disquieting questions of its own. Had such a sham arrangement deprived her of what a real marriage might have offered? She had always scoffed at Robbie's suggestion that a man might inspire her to dream girlish dreams. Or, even more improbably, to fall in love. But was it such an absurd notion?

A sigh escaped from somewhere deep inside as she thought about the encircling strength of Alex's arm around her shoulders. It had been comforting to nestle up against his chest, savoring the corded ripple of muscle, the texture of his dark locks against her cheek, and the faint woodsy tang of his person. He made her feel . . . safe. Yet at the same time, he also stirred strange longings that were decidedly dangerous to her old way of thinking.

All of a sudden, Aurora found she wanted someone to lean on when clouds threatened to obscure Orion and all the other constellations. More disturbing yet, the mere thought of his touch was causing her to grow warm in places she had never thought about before. The physical aspect of marriage, as described by the women of her acquaintance, had always sounded more of an onerous chore than anything that might prove a pleasant experience. But now she found she was curious. Insatiably curious to know what it would be like to have Alex do some of the things she had seen depicted in that enticing little book of his.

May Lucifer's wings be singed. It was all so very confusing! Robbie's novels had made love seem simple and straightforward. What she was feeling was neither, so she couldn't possibly be in love with Alex Woodmore.

The devilish question was . . .

Enough! Even an idiot could see how hopelessly foolish it would be to let her thoughts keep wandering in such a direction. With a grimace of irony, her mouth pursed into a semblance of a smile, mocking such naive longings. She prided herself on possessing at least a modicum of intelligence, and it was clear that if she was going to fall in love with any man, it had better be her husband, else the consequences would only lead to disaster. And since the chance of *that* happening was only marginally greater than that of her replacing Castlereagh as prime minister, her heart had best remain unmoved! No matter what turmoil the rest of her body and brain were in.

A squall of wind suddenly caused the rough-planked front door to fly open, and Aurora hurried over to close it. As her fingers worked to secure the rusting latch, she warned herself that she must do the same with her own unsettled emotions. They must be locked away, at least for now.

There would be plenty of long, empty nights to think about what sweet dreams might have been possible, had the cards that life had dealt fallen in her favor.

Chapter Nine

The weather began to mirror her bleak feelings. A swirl of fog eddied around the cottage while a series of rain showers beat an intermittent tattoo against the weathered stone. With a slight shiver, Aurora added another log to the dying fire, trying to ward off a chill of foreboding.

Oh, stop waxing melodramatic! She took a deep breath as flames leaped up from the embers and cast a welcome glow of light over the hearth. The prose—and pictures—of the volume she had been reading were starting to affect her reason. It was time to put such storybook nonsense aside and return to behaving in her normal, sensible fashion rather than like an impressionable schoolroom miss. Still, the rest of the room seemed shrouded in an ominous gloom and she couldn't help but slant a nervous glance behind her, half expecting to catch a glimpse of some mad monk skulking in the flickering shadows.

What she did spy, carefully closed with its cords drawn tight, was the bag of Alex's belongings. Her eyes lingered on the weathered canvas. What secrets lay inside?

What sort of personal matters did he wish to keep hidden away? His reticence was hardly to be wondered at, she supposed, for a man in his profession must learn to be guarded, and trusting in others could be dangerous.

Her lips quirked up. *Rather like herself.*

But there were other qualities about Alex that had surprised her. One might have expected a seasoned soldier to be hard and unbending, charging forward with weapons drawn and nary a waver to his step. Yet there was more to him than that. On further acquaintance he had proved to be a man of great complexity, a strange mix of steel tempered with compassion and kindness. Indeed, he seemed to have as many facets as the jewel whose color his eyes so resembled. And as with the precious stone from the East, the light winked and flashed off all his surfaces, but the real essence remained somehow elusive.

A mystery.

Aurora poked at the fire with a snort of disgust. Lord, her vivid imagination was threatening to turn this whole evening into a chapter worthy of Mrs. Radcliffe's pen. There was no need to act as flighty as one of those pea-goose heroines. Nor was it sensible to make Alex Woodmore into some brooding, sensitive hero when he was merely a well-trained British officer intent on accomplishing a difficult mission. Gritting her teeth at the very idea of acting like such a ninny, she forced herself to retreat to the other room to comb out her curls and don her nightrail.

It was eminently reasonable to be cool, calm, and detached about the whole thing. She would simply crawl beneath the covers of her pallet and fall asleep. By morning, the matter would be settled and they could all get back to the normal course of their lives. Her head settled against the thin pillow, and at the thought of returning to her snug little cottage and Robbie's comfortable companionship, a sigh stole forth from her lips. It was prompted by a sense of relief, she assured herself as her eyes squeezed shut, and not by any other sentiment.

No more than a quarter of an hour later, a sharp noise caused her head to shoot up. *Was that the snap of a branch or the crack of a pistol?* Muttering several choice words under her breath, she punched at the pillow and turned on her side. Wind rustled the leaves—or was it the sound of an approaching rider? This time, the unladylike oath was more than audible. Abandoning all pretense of sleep, she rose and wrapped one of the thin blankets around her shoulders, then returned to her pacing before the dying embers.

The faint stirrings of warmth did nothing to loosen the cold knot of worry that had formed in the pit of her stomach. *What if he has taken another bullet and lies wounded in some ditch?* Her fingers clenched at the rough wool. She must stop such worrying! Not only did it do no good, but she would likely be teased unmercifully if he returned to find her lapsing into a state of girlish vapors.

Or what if the blade of a knife has . . .

A rasping of metal caused her head to jerk around toward the door, but the cry of alarm gave way to one of welcome as the tall figure who slipped inside shook the drops of rain from his coat, the familiar set of shoulders unmarred by any trace of injury.

"Here now, since I've managed to avoid being shot or stabbed earlier tonight, I would prefer not to be strangled at the last minute," he said gently, though he made no move to unclasp her arms from around his neck.

Aurora buried her cheek against his damp shirt, but the tart rejoinder to his teasing dissolved into a burbled sob.

A light caress brushed over her loosened hair. "It's all right, sweeting," he whispered. "It's over."

Her eyes flew up. "You—Jack—"

"Both of us are fine. And thanks to your help, the threat to our country is at an end as well." He took both her hands in his and led her to the table. "I shall tell you all, but first, perhaps, you might fetch that flask from your reticule. I think we could both use a medicinal draught." A glint of amusement cut through the fatigue in his eyes. "That is, unless it really did break along with the bottle of vinaigrette. But I sincerely hope not."

Aurora could not deny that the fiery brandy did indeed send a jolt of warmth through her insides, but it was not nearly as potent as the heat caused by the closeness of his person. She passed the flask back to him and watched as he raised it to his lips and took a long swallow before speaking again.

"It went very much as we had planned," he began in a low voice. "Jack trailed the two of them from the small inn to the only cove where a boat might put in with any safety. I was already well hidden among the rocks, and we took them by surprise, just as they were beginning the steep descent down to the water's edge. Our friend from the inn tried to draw his weapon, but Jack dropped him with a single shot." He paused and took another draught. "The lady, on seeing she was trapped, attempted no such resistance. She merely gave me a strange sort of smile—almost a salute— and simply . . . stepped over the edge." His fingers sought out a sheaf of papers from inside his shirt. They were torn in several places and bore faint but unmistakable streaks of blood across the crumpled foolscap. "A pity such courage and cunning could not have been put to better use," he said with a trace of weary sadness in his voice. "Her accomplice was only winged. Jack is seeing to the man's wounds, and to having the local magistrate take care of the other body without raising any awkward questions. He will spend the night in the village to make sure the incident is hushed up; then in the morning he'll head off to London with his prisoner. Perhaps with thorough questioning we'll find some sort of answer for all the blood that has been shed. But I doubt it." For a moment his eyes pressed closed and Aurora was shocked by the spasm of pain that tugged at his features.

"You . . . have not become used to the sight of death?"

"No. And I hope that I never shall." His gaze strayed to the few flames that still licked up from the glowing coals. "Death is a terrible waste. It serves to remind me that life is infinitely precious, though I have been wont to fritter it away as casually as a drunken gambler tosses his blunt down on the table of chance."

The note of regret in his voice caused Aurora to reach out and catch up his hand. "You, of all people, have too much integrity to have ever allowed your dreams to be bought or sold in such a frivolous manner. Of that I am sure."

"Are you?" A muscle twitched at his jaw. "Soldiers are a mercenary lot," he replied with some bitterness, seeking to free his fingers from her grasp. "Aurora Sprague, you don't know the first thing about me."

The blanket had slipped from her shoulders as he sought to pull away. Ignoring the fact that nothing but a thin layer of white lawn cotton covered the swell of her breasts, Aurora refused to be brushed aside so easily. "I may have no knowledge of whatever past mistakes or triumphs or disasters have shaped your character, but I have seen enough of you to know what good qualities lurk within your heart, no matter how much you seek to keep them a secret." Her mouth had ended up only inches from his. "I-I hadn't thought it likely that there existed a male whose overweening conceit and bullying nature did not overshadow any—"

Alex did not allow her to finish. His lips came down upon hers, cutting off all words save for an inarticulate cry from deep in her throat. With an answering groan of passion, he was all of a sudden on his feet, the table knocked over on its side as he gathered her in his arms.

"I fear I don't deserve your high opinion, but I am weak enough to accept it, because I want it very badly." His hand was cupping one of her breasts, his fingers coaxing the rosy tip to a throbbing hardness. "I want it very badly, indeed," he murmured, lowering his head to take the nub and a swirl of sheer fabric between his teeth.

Aurora feared that for the first time in her life she might swoon. Only the thought that she would then be unconscious to the glorious things he was doing to her body kept her senses from going completely blank. She arched under his touch, her knees clenched around his thigh to keep her legs from careening off in opposite directions. The soft cries that filled the darkened room echoed with an urgent need she would never have recognized as her own, having never experienced it before.

Her hands clung to the damp linen of his shirt, then loosened the fastenings and slid inside, her palms running over the coarse curls and bare skin. His own low moans mingled with the sounds of her passion, and suddenly her nightrail was lifted up and over her head, leaving her completely naked to the rovings of his touch.

"Sweet Jesus," he whispered hoarsely, yanking off his own shirt so that she might explore the breadth of him. They had somehow moved to the far side of the hearth and Alex slowly lowered their entwined bodies down onto the pallet that had served as his bed. "Has it been a long time since you have been with a man, sweeting?" he asked, as his mouth grazed over one nipple, then the other.

She nodded, finding it impossible to speak any coherent word.

"Then I shall try to go slowly." He sat up and tugged off his boots with barely concealed impatience. "Though in truth I feel no more in control than a randy schoolboy about to have his first experience at lovemaking." His breeches followed and he turned to straddle her, as unclothed as she was.

In answer, she reached up and pulled his head down,

opening her mouth in intimate invitation for him to enter
her. Their tongues touched in a heated embrace, and Aurora
felt something ignite in the core of her being. His hand left
a trail of sparks along the soft planes of her belly, and when
it came to rest at the downy triangle between her legs, she
was positively on fire.

Her voice cried out—for what she wasn't sure. But Alex
seemed to have no trouble interpreting her need. His fingers
began a slow, circular caress, and for a moment she thought
she might go up in smoke.

"Alex. Oh, *Alex,*" she moaned, nipping at the tanned
flesh of his neck.

"Has your husband never pleasured you in such a way?"
he demanded, increasing both the rhythm and intensity of
his touch.

"N-n-no."

"Then he should be cursed as a lout as well as a fool," he
growled.

"Please I I do not wish to speak of my husband," she
whispered.

"Nor do I, sweeting. I don't intend for you to think of *any*
man save me at this moment." Aurora gasped as he slipped
a finger inside her passage. "Lord, you are ready for me, and
I-I can wait no longer." With a slow thrust of his hips, he
buried his shaft deep within her.

She flinched, a small squeak escaping her lips. Alex
made a startled sound of his own and withdrew with a hurried jerk. Stunned, he stared at the trace of blood. "Why, you
are . . . an innocent," he exclaimed, his voice rough with
both shock and desire.

"I-I suppose that means you don't want me either," she
replied, turning her head so he could not see the tears
welling up in her eyes.

"Don't want you?" he repeated in some confusion.

"Yes! There is always something about me that puts men

off. I am too opinionated, too independent, too headstrong. And now, it seems, too inexperienced."

She tried to squirm out from beneath him, but he kept her firmly down against the rumpled sheet. "You think I don't want you? That I am in some way . . . upset that you have known no other man's touch?" When she didn't answer, he took her face in both hands and tilted it so that she could not avoid meeting his eyes. The color of blue in them was smoky, as if he, too, was alight with some inner fire. His lips possessed a searing heat as well, as they slowly traced a path across each cheekbone. "I have never wanted a woman as much as I want you right now." He fanned her hair out over the pillow and twined his fingers in the silky curls before taking her mouth in another long, lingering kiss.

"R-really?" Aurora touched his chin and gave a tentative smile. "You aren't going to . . . stop, then?"

"I could not stop myself now, no more than I could stop the sun from tinging the horizon with the glorious light of a new day, my sweet Aurora." He entered her again, with great care, and began a slow, gentle rocking. "You must tell me if I am hurting you."

Her hands clung to his muscled shoulders. "Oh no! Alex, it feels . . ." Her words drifted off as she started to match his rhythm. A husky chuckle tickled her ear. "What, no adjectives come to mind? Let me see if I might make you think of one or two." Urging her legs to wrap around his hips, he sparked a hotter pace to their union. Soon she was in flames again.

A jolt of heat surged through her, then suddenly exploded with a shuddering flash of light. "Divine," she mouthed against his stubbled cheek, feeling indeed as if she had just ascended to heaven. She heard him cry out, too, a hoarse, elemental sound as he buried himself to the hilt and achieved his own release.

Then they lay still, joined as one, and she could feel the

warmth of his passion deep within her, hear the pounding of his heart over the racing of her own pulse, and taste the salty tang of exertion upon his skin.

Rather than engendering any sense of loss, the surrender of her maidenhood made her feel strangely . . . whole.

Alex twined a length of her hair around his fingers and held it up to the faint glow of the flickering coals, reveling in the subtle nuances of color. It reminded him of Aurora herself. Each shift of light seemed to reveal a new and intriguing shade. With such infinite possibilities, he couldn't imagine that it would ever become boring to behold. His gaze shifted to her face. The same was true for her person. Eyes closed, she lay with her head to one side, the shadowed profile of her strong features in silhouette against the lighter covering of the pillow.

She was without question the most compelling female he had ever met, this young lady whose life had become so inextricably intertwined with his own. Already he had discovered so much beneath the surface of her scowls and sharp words. There were courage, intelligence, sensitivity, and, finally, a depth of passion that had left his senses rather singed. Surely it would take a lifetime, at the very least, to begin to fathom the depths of her character—

His jaw tightened. He had no right to think in such terms. Neither of them were free to contemplate any future beyond the next dawn.

She stirred, and with an odd sense of loss, he shifted the length of his spent body to one side, then cuddled her close to his bare chest. Good Lord, he liked the feeling of her warmth against him, and the fresh scent of lavender and sunshine that wafted up from her skin.

A sigh caught in his throat. He supposed he should feel some measure of guilt or shame at deflowering another man's wife. But he didn't. The only emotion coursing through him was a fierce, primeval exultation, coupled with a desire to keep her safe, encircled in the protection of his arms. Whatever the law said, she was his in some irrevocable way. Nothing could change that.

Her eyes opened and a shy smile came to her lips. "Alex Woodmore," she murmured, venturing to run her fingers through the dark curls on his breast. "I had always thought men selfish, caring only for themselves, but you are . . . so different. With your strength and compassion, you have shown me that the notion of honor is indeed more than a hollow word."

It was as if a knife had been plunged in his gut.

"I had always thought men supremely arrogant as well," she continued. "But you are not afraid to ask for help or to receive it. Nor are you pompous—you have a wonderful sense of humor and most importantly, you can laugh at yourself." She settled her cheek at the base of his throat. For a moment there was silence, save for the whisper of her breathing; then she went on in a halting voice. "For the first time, I find myself wishing to know if my so-called husband is still alive. So that I might know whether—I am free."

He had only to remain silent, he told himself. Surely it was not so very wrong to let her believe that if not for her own situation he might . . . *No!* She had suffered enough betrayals at the hands of men. He could not offer false promises, not even if they were unspoken rather than any overt lies.

His hand came up to brush a loose tendril from her forehead. "Sweeting"—the words nearly stuck in his throat— "there is something you should know. I . . . I am married as well."

*   *   *

.

Aurora became utterly still. Then, after the initial shock had
passed, she mustered all of her considerable resolve and
managed to make an even reply. "I see."

His body was all of sudden like a block of ice, its touch
chilling her to the very marrow. Suppressing a shiver, she
jerked away. Her head turned to stare into the black shadows
so he could not see the look of utter desolation that quivered
on her features, or the tears that threatened to spill down her
cheeks.

Alex has a wife!

No doubt it was her love letters tucked away in his bag
that he had been guarding so zealously. And the book! No
wonder he had been angry. The book was no military
code—it was really meant for her, too. Or rather, the two of
them. He used it to remind himself of all the delectable
things he meant to do with her when he finally returned
home from the sordid business of war.

Aurora bit at her lip so hard she nearly drew blood. Of
course he had a home. And *she* was there, ready to welcome
him from the battlefields, ready to cook his meals, wash his
shirts . . . and warm his bed. Lord, he probably had children
as well, eager to pull at his long legs and tickle his chin.
Somehow the thought of a dark-haired little boy or girl with
sapphire blue eyes and a crooked smile was almost too
much to bear.

He had a real home and a real family. She had . . . neither.

How could I have been such a bloody, bloody fool! How
could she have been gulled into thinking Alex was different
from other males. And how could he have led her to believe
she was more than just an amusing diversion during a rather
grim mission? Now that that duty was done, it was clear he
was quite ready to put all thought of it—and her—out of his
mind. The heartless wretch!

It seemed she needn't have searched so hard for adjectives to describe him, for the usual ones would suit quite nicely. *"Selfish." "Manipulative." "Philandering."*

Well, it would not be the first time a man had taken advantage of her. As on the previous occasions, anger gave her the strength to shore up her crumbling heart.

"Aurora . . ." he began hesitantly.

"If you think you must offer some flowery apology, don't bother," she said in a brittle voice. "After all, what does it matter?"

"I-I never lied to you."

"Oh, quite right, sir." Her voice was sharp with sarcasm. "You took great care that such an accusation could not be laid at your door."

Alex reached out, but she stiffened at the first graze of his fingers and shifted to avoid his touch. In some confusion, he let his hand fall away. "I'm sorry," he faltered. "You must believe I never meant to hurt—"

But he had! She wanted to bury her head against his shoulder and drown her pain in a flood of tears. She wanted to wrap her arms around his waist and have him fill the aching emptiness inside her. She wanted to take his face between her hands and have him tell her he . . .

Instead, she forced a harsh laugh to interrupt his words. "I can hardly castigate you, sir, for your infidelity. After all, I am also just a common adulteress, so we both should be ashamed of our actions tonight. But perhaps such an inconvenient emotion goes away with practice. You would know better than I." She paused to draw in a ragged breath. "Tell me, does your wife know of your affairs? Or, like most females, does she simply accept it as the way men are? Perhaps she is content, as long as your occasional attentions leave her dewy-eyed and round with your child." Hating the bitterness that had seeped into her voice, she bit off any further words.

Aurora heard him give a harried sigh. "It's not like that at all. I . . ."

She waited, but he didn't continue. "You what?"

He still didn't answer.

Feeling raw and awkward in her nakedness, she clutched one of the rumpled blankets to her breast and then stood up. "Good night, sir. I am tired and wish to seek some sleep. After all, both of us have had a trying day."

He let her go, unable to wrap his tongue around any explanation that might give her cause to stay. Would she have thought any better of him had he admitted to the truth of his marriage? That he had used such solemn vows to gain his own ends, without a passing thought for the female who had been left trapped in the leg shackle?

Not bloody likely!

And he could hardly blame her, for he wasn't feeling much in charity with himself either, regardless of the fact that the circumstances of his nuptials had been none of his own choosing. In many ways, he knew he was no better than her own lout of a husband for shirking his responsibilities, even though it hadn't been until she had made him see things from a different perspective that he had realized how damnable his own actions had been.

Turning onto his back, Alex stared up at the sooty, rough-hewn beams, a wry grimace causing his lips to purse. *Hell's teeth!* Now that he thought about it, there was something else he and her husband had in common. Neither of them had bothered to consummate his marriage before abandoning it for self-proclaimed freedom. It was an odd coincidence, but . . .

The thought was dismissed with a shrug. Of the two of them, he, at least, had made up his mind to seek some measure of redress for the injured party. His supposed wife deserved another chance at finding happiness, even if he did not. As soon as he got to London, he vowed his first order of business as the Earl of Woodbridge would be to see about arranging an annulment. With his new wealth and title, it should not prove too difficult. He doubted the countess would have much of an objection, not when she was presented with the generous settlement he meant to provide for her.

Once he was free, truly free, perhaps he might hope . . .

Might hope what? That Mr. Sprague no longer existed? Or that if he did, he could be convinced to grant Aurora an annulment? His lips compressed in a grim line. Is that what he wanted? His breath came out in a ragged sigh. Lord, he hadn't even begun to sort out his feelings regarding her, much less make any sense out of them. And in any case, he was rushing his fences. Maybe the first thing he had better hope for was that Aurora did not hate him.

But perhaps if she knew the full story, and what amends he meant to make for his sordid past, she would find it in her heart to forgive him. At least he must venture a try, for what he had left unsaid had caused a wound too grievous to heal by itself. His own tongue-tied embarrassment had caused her to think yet another male had simply used her for his own amusement, then cast her aside, as a child would a toy whose performance had paled or part had cracked.

Nor must she, on any account, be left to believe he had a real marriage, with a willing wife and doting children. He had caught a glimpse of her face, despite the shadows. The thought of such a betrayal had been like a knife in the back. The hurt of it, if left to fester, would slowly cause the life in her to take sick and die, leaving nothing but a brittle, withered shell.

First thing in the morning, he would make her listen to the truth. In doing so he would be abandoning all his soldierly instincts and making himself vulnerable to another person. Yet somehow, the idea of exposing his weaknesses to her was not as frightening as he had imagined. He had long ago ceased to think of Aurora as he did other females. Rather than seeing her as the enemy, he considered her more as a friend, a trusted comrade in arms.

Good Lord, what a muddle. But he was too exhausted to think on it any further. Trusting that dawn would help shed a fresh light on things, he drifted off into a deep, dreamless sleep.

Chapter Ten

The shadow angled across the pillow, revealing that the morning was quickly advancing toward noon. Still half asleep, Alex winced and ran a hand through his tangled locks as he sat up. A dull ache throbbed at his temples, and no amount of rubbing seemed able to banish the nagging discomfort. It took a moment for his gaze to focus on the trail of his discarded clothing scattered across the floor and the rumpled disorder of the bedding, where the faint scent of their passion still clung to the sheet. A low oath slipped out from between his gritted teeth as the details of the previous night came flooding back. No wonder he felt like the devil. It was a long fall from heaven to hell.

Aurora.

There was no sign of life from within her room. A second look around showed that the hearth lay cold, the larder had not been opened, and the table had not yet been righted onto its rickety legs. Fighting off a sense of foreboding, he stumbled to his feet and tugged on his breeches. Then, heedless

of his bare calves and chest, he crossed to the closed door
and gave an urgent knock.

"Aurora?"

He called again, softly but with an edge of concern. Still
nothing. After a slight hesitation, he opened the door and entered.

"Damnation!"

This time the word echoed off the thick stones with the
force of a pistol shot. Every item she possessed was gone.
Pausing only long enough to yank on his boots and snatch
up his shirt, he raced outside and headed toward the river.
Perhaps she was merely tidying up, he told himself, yet even
to his own ears the suggestion rang hollow. He had covered
only a short distance when his steps slowed, then came to a
dead halt. There was but a single horse tethered in the
meadow. The mount that Jack had purchased a few days ago
was nowhere to be seen. For a few moments he stood and
simply stared out at the rippling meadow grasses and low-
lying bushes of gorse. It was impossible to deny the truth of
it any longer.

She had left. And he had no idea where she had gone.

Forcing himself to turn back toward the cottage, Alex
tried to sort out what options lay open to him. It took precious little time for his jaw to tighten. Actually, there were
none. Given her head start, Aurora could be at any number of coaching inns, or already on her way south. He
could hardly begin to search the entire southwest corner of
Scotland, not with Whitehall expecting immediate deliv-
ery of the documents he held and a full report on the mission.

Duty demanded that he make all haste for London. Once
he had exchanged the rank of major for the title of earl, he
would be free to make his own choices. That is, if he could
figure out just who he really was and what he really wanted.

A gust had blown the heavy oak door shut. He reached

out, but instead of taking hold of the iron latch, his fist slammed into the rough wood with as much force as he could muster. The bloodied knuckles and splintered skin only served to remind him that physical pain was not nearly as difficult to bear as what he was feeling inside.

Miss Robertson pushed her spectacles back to the bridge of her nose and regarded the state of her former charge's appearance. "Well, if you don't look just like something the cat dragged in and spent half the night making sport with."

It was an unfortunate analogy. Aurora's lower lip quivered slightly as she tucked a loose tendril behind her ear and tossed her dusty reticule onto the top of her desk. "How kind of you to point it out," she snapped. "But given my current mood, if Homer—or any other male beast—flexes his furried claws within a twenty paces of me, I vow I shall kick in his teeth."

The older woman made a sympathetic clucking sound. "Oh dear, were you forced to endure the company of a particularly vexing man for part of the journey?" She came over to plant a light kiss on Aurora's wan cheek. "I knew I shouldn't have let you go off by yourself, especially after the duchess's coachman delivered that vague note announcing an unavoidable delay. However, you may put the experience all behind you now that you are back among friends. I am sure you will feel like new after a hot bath and a slice of Alice's apple tart." Her ample arm went around Aurora's sagging shoulders. "Welcome home, my dear."

Aurora looked around the familiar little room and burst into tears.

"What do you mean you can't find her!" The new Earl of Woodbridge was perilously close to shouting.

His man of affairs blotted the sheen of perspiration from his forehead with the cuff of his jacket. "Er, well, my lord, apparently no one ever informed either of us that she never took up residence at Rexford."

"Never?"

The fellow gave a nervous swallow, then shook his head. "It appears not."

"But she does receive the quarterly draft of funds?"

"Yes, my lord. We haven't yet tracked down exactly where it goes or how it gets there, but we are working on the matter."

Alex paused in his pacing before the ornately carved mantel of his town house library. "Well, keep at it!" He raked an impatient hand through his locks, achieving a result that would have caused his new valet to fall into a fit of vapors had he observed it. "In the meantime, Perkins, try sending a letter in the same manner as the money." Under his breath he added, "Perhaps a penny stamp will prove more effective than the barrow full of blunt I am paying you and your minions."

"An excellent suggestion, my lord! I'll get right on it." Pouncing on the opportunity to make good his escape, the man bowed and scurried from the room.

Alex heaved a sigh, then moved to the massive claw-footed desk and rang for his butler to usher in the last of his morning appointments.

"A Mr. Swallow to see you, my lord." The starchy servant ended his words with a slight sniff, indicating what he thought of the sort of visitor the new earl was allowing to set foot in the polished halls of Woodbridge House. "Says he has been requested to make an appearance before you."

"Show him in, Huggins."

The sight of the stooped, reedy figure who shuffled his worn boots across the expensive Aubusson carpet was hard to reconcile with the assurances he had received that the man was the best that Bow Street had to offer. However, Alex had had a good deal of experience in judging the true merits of a man. As soon as the fellow turned his sharp gaze from the expensive appointments of the room to meet that of his prospective employer, the new earl caught sight of the intelligence lurking within the half-closed eyes and was encouraged.

"G'day, m'lord." The Runner twisted a greasy cap between his fingers. "Colonel Wilbourne seems te think I may be of use t'you."

"I'm told you have some skill at tracking down a missing person, no matter how slight the clues," demanded Alex without any preamble.

The man didn't waver under the earl's piercing stare. "Aye. If there's breath left in a body, I'll find yer man."

Alex motioned for the man to step closer to the desk. Unfolding a large map, drawn to scale, he took up a piece of string tied to a pen. After dipping the nib in red ink, he held one end of the string down on the center of London, then inscribed a bold circle atop the fine lines and shadings. "That is a radius of one hundred and fifty miles from Town," he said, tossing the implements aside. "You will follow that path, stopping at every blasted town or village or hamlet if you must, until you discover the location of the Sprague Agency for Distressed Females."

The Runner's sharp features remained impassive, but his eyes took on a gleam of interest. "Hmm. Not quite yer ordinary butcher, baker, or candlestick maker. I take it ye want me te locate this Sprague?"

"I do."

"And?"

"Just find her."

The man's brow quirked up slightly at the use of the pronoun.

"The quickest way to get any information is to speak with

a barmaid or charwoman or the like," continued Alex. "Oh, and you had best pretend you are the loyal retainer of some persecuted female in need of some . . . professional assistance. That's the only way you will get them to talk."

Mr. Swallow scratched at his chin as he regarded the map. "Hmm. 'Tis a weighty task."

" 'Tis a weighty purse." Alex tossed a heavy leather bag down next to the creased paper. "Inside is a note detailing the rest of the particulars. Can you handle the job, Mr. Swallow?"

A small smile creased the man's thin lips. "What did this Sprague woman do—purloin the family jewels?"

Alex scowled. "Just find her, Mr. Swallow. Can you do that?"

"Oh, aye. And it sounds a mite more interesting than pursuing the usual murderer or embezzler." He put the map in his pocket, along with the bulge of gold guineas. "Don't worry, m'lord. I'll find her. But it may take some time."

"Then I suggest you waste not a minute more. There's a hefty bonus in it for you if the task is accomplished quickly."

The Runner bobbed his head and made for the door without further delay.

"Damnation," growled Alex after the man had left. He sat down and began to twist the ebony pen in his fingers, heedless of the spatter of scarlet that fell onto one cuff. There was nothing he could do now except wait.

"Good Lord! What's wrong, Robbie?"

The former governess uttered another word that was definitely not taught in any schoolroom and looked up from the letter lying in her lap. "It's from . . . the Earl of Woodbridge."

For an instant there was a flicker of hope in Aurora's

eyes, though it died away just as quickly. *Don't be a fool,* she chided herself. *And a rather heartless one at that.* Despite her joking, she did not truly wish for another person's death. Besides, even if the current missive contained the news of her husband's demise, it would not change things in the least.

She bent back over the report she was writing up for the duchess and feigned a casual indifference to the letter's contents. "I thought my dear father-in-law had passed away some years ago."

"He did."

"So what does the current earl want?"

"Er." Miss Robertson cleared her throat. "He wants to meet with his wife."

"What!" Abandoning all pretense of unconcern, Aurora bolted up from her chair and snatched the crested stationery from the folds of muslin.

The older woman's hands knitted together in a tight ball as Aurora skimmed through the sheets of paper. "I had read that the eldest son was killed in a carriage accident, but, well, I gave it little thought. The news of the next one's death must have been printed during that little spell when we decided to forego the expense of the newspaper." She watched the scowl on her former charge's face became blacker with every sentence that was read. "Oh dear, what a bumble broth! W-what do you intend to do, my dear?"

Aurora's lips curled into a sardonic smile. "Now that the preening prig is a high and mighty lord, it's obvious he wishes to look elsewhere for a bride." Her gaze fell down once more to the closely spaced lines of elegant copperplate script. "He wants his freedom, does he? Well, that suits me just fine, especially as he is willing to pay handsomely for it." With a curt laugh she stuffed the letter into the pocket of her gown. "Come, Robbie, you have always said that you wished to visit London above all things. And so have I. Let's start packing."

Within the week, the two of them were comfortably settled in Town. The earl's man of affairs had responded to Aurora's quickly penned reply by arranging everything. An elderly Woodbridge aunt was away taking the cure at Bath and her town house was put at their disposal, along with a good deal more servants than Aurora or Miss Robertson considered necessary. Before either of them could think to demur, they were whisked off to a series of fittings with the most sought-after modiste in London, and a selection of open accounts at the finest shops on Bond Street were made available. When questioned, the man of affairs simply stated that he was following His Lordship's specific orders.

"You have to admit that the current Lord Woodbridge appears not to be a nip cheese like his father. Or yours," remarked Miss Robertson, fingering the soft wool of her new day gown as she watched yet another pile of boxes being carried up the marble stairs. "He has been most generous in insisting that we acquire a suitable wardrobe and other necessaries for our stay in Town."

Aurora glanced down at her own figured silk skirts. "You may be seduced by a few fripperies, Robbie," she muttered. "But the rogue is going to have to cough up a good deal more than that if he wishes to get what he wants from me."

The former governess's cheeks turned quite pink. "Seduction is quite the furthest thought from my mind—"

"From mine as well." Aurora grinned. "I am far more interested in the notion of extortion. How much do you think I should attempt to squeeze out of him this first time around?"

Miss Robertson gave a strangled cough. "My dear, pray do try to moderate your opinions somewhat when meeting your—that is, Lord Woodbridge for the first time. Surely it would help make things go as you wish if you make some attempt to be civil to the man."

Aurora said something under her breath that the older woman did not ask her to repeat.

With a purse of her lips, Miss Robertson regarded her former charge's rigid profile and the defiant tilt of her jaw. "Are you sure you do not wish for me to accompany you to the meeting? I—"

"No, I prefer to go alone. There's nothing to be concerned about. I can handle the situation just fine on my own."

"Hmmph! As I recall, that's what you said the last time you went haring off without me."

Aurora had the grace to color slightly. "This is entirely different," she muttered through gritted teeth. "I am going to meet with my husband and his solicitors, not with—"

"Not with some dashing, rakish major with eyes the color of jewels?" Miss Robertson crossed her arms over her ample chest and gave another snort. "Hmmph! Well, let us hope there are not *two* such men on this earth who could have such an effect on your fluttering heart."

"Oh, do stop sounding as if you are reading a passage from *The Mysteries of Udolpho*." Aurora turned away to gaze out of the tall mullioned windows of the drawing room. "The major had *no* effect on my heart, save to cause it to heat my blood to the boiling point." She bit her lip. "With anger, of course."

Miss Robertson refrained from making any direct reply and simply reached over to give Aurora a quick hug. A harried sigh followed. "Men! Detestable creatures!"

The slight tremble on Aurora's lips turned into a laugh. "Oh, Robbie, whatever would I do without your stalwart support and keen sense of humor!" She picked up her new reticule from the gilt side table. "But truly, you have no need to worry. I think my heart has learned its lesson regarding rakish soldiers. If the Earl of Woodbridge thinks he can use any sort of wiles on me, he had better think twice. He has no idea who he is up against."

Alex took a deep breath and adjusted the precise folds of his cravat yet again. "She has arrived?"

"Yes, my lord." His man of affairs shifted the hefty portfolio of legal papers from one arm to another. "I have just brought her in to meet the fellow you had me hire to handle her part of the proceedings. I suppose we had best give them a few minutes to review the matter in private before we join them."

Alex clasped his hands behind his back, then shifted his weight from foot to foot. "Perkins . . ."

"Yes, my lord."

"Er, my experience as a soldier has taught me it is a wise thing to have engaged in some, er, reconnaissance before entering enemy territory."

"Sir?"

This was damned awkward, he fumed to himself, but he couldn't quite overcome a sudden curiosity. "Er, you are aware of the circumstances of my marriage, since you helped my father draw up the agreement. It was a long time ago, and I was not exactly in full possession of my faculties during our one meeting . . . " There was a fraction of a pause. "So tell me, is she . . . short and stout?"

The man coughed. "Rather tall and slender."

"Dark mousy hair?"

"Light, my lord. Not exactly blond, but . . ."

"Attractive?"

The man took a moment to extract a handkerchief from his pocket and dab at his forehead. "What one man may find—"

"Don't prevaricate, man. I wish an honest answer."

"Yes. Quite."

Alex twisted at the gold signet ring on his finger and muttered something under his breath. "One last question—"

A discreet knock on the paneled door interrupted the earl's words. Looking greatly relieved, Perkins swallowed hard and took hold of the polished brass knob. "I believe they are ready, my lord."

But am I? asked Alex as he followed the other man into the next room. It was not that he had any doubts as to whether his decision was the right one. It was just that now, after so many years of not giving a thought to the lady who bore his name, he found himself strangely nervous at the idea of coming face-to-face with her. Rather like a groom approaching the noose, he added with gallows humor, rather than one seeking to cut the knot that bound the two of them for life.

Her back was to him. Even from that angle, it was clear Perkins had not exaggerated her charms. His wife was indeed tall and willowy, with a mass of silky curls artfully arranged to spill down her back in a simple twist. The stylish cut of her emerald figured silk gown accentuated a slender waist, smoothly rounded shoulders, and the graceful arc of her neck. Alex suddenly felt his throat constrict. *The Devil take it!* She reminded him so much of a certain other young lady that for an instant it was impossible to breathe.

His step faltered, and he gave a prolonged mental curse, chiding himself for being a complete and utter fool. The memory of Aurora seemed to haunt his every move these days. Why, he heard her laugh in the box at the Opera, recognized the exact shade of her hair in the shimmer of silk at a fancy ball, saw the shape of her chin in a Gainsborough painting over his mantel. And right now, he could swear he heard the soft whisper of her voice murmuring . . .

This was insane! Alex fought to recover some measure of

control. He must stop acting like a moonstruck halfling and concentrate on business. The business of sundering all ties with the stranger before him. Clearing his throat, he forced himself to speak in a firm voice.

"Perhaps, if Lady Woodbridge is ready, we might begin."

He thought he detected a spasm run through her at his first words. Somehow, the idea that she might well be as nervous as he was helped ease some of the tension in his clenched jaw. "Mr. Perkins has provided you with a copy of the necessary legal papers and the proposed settlement—"

She turned to face him, and all at once the rest of what he was saying was drowned out by an odd roaring sound that began in his ears and threatened to engulf the rest of his senses.

The silence in the room was deafening. Alex was aware that his lips had stopped moving, as had every other part of him. She, too, stood absolutely motionless, her emerald eyes mirroring the same shock and surprise that must have been evident in his own startled gaze.

Blithely unaware of the tension that had descended over the room, the other man of affairs put down his folder of documents on the large oaken table and pulled out a chair for his client. The rasp of its legs across the polished boards seemed to break the spell. Aurora quickly looked away and sat down without a word. Perkins slanted a look of concern at the earl before taking a place opposite the others. Somehow, the thought that the fashionable reticule looped around her wrist probably contained a new bottle of vinaigrette allowed Alex to gain his own chair without making a cake of himself by falling in a most unlordly swoon.

There was a rustle of papers. Several clerks appeared, armed with fresh foolscap, quills, and ink. At a sign from Perkins, they seated themselves at either end of the long table. The advisor hired for Aurora, a distinguished-looking older man by the name of Seymour, took a moment to clean his spectacles. As he did so, she leaned over and whispered something in his ear. His brows rose a fraction, but he nodded and turned to face his colleague.

"Er, before we begin, my client and I should like to clarify one rather basic fact. Mr. Perkins, can you vouch that the gentleman seated at your right is"—Aurora repeated something in a low whisper—"is indeed James Fenimore?"

Perkins nodded his assent. "Yes. Since I have known him from the time he was in leading strings, I can state unequivocally that this is James Hadley Alexander Fenimore. Third son of the late Deverall George Eustace Fenimore, the sixth earl of Woodbridge, and the lawfully wedded spouse of one Elizabeth Jane Aurora Taft. Now a Fenimore herself, of course."

Aurora's lips compressed in a tight line and she leaned back in her chair without further comment.

Seymour shot a questioning look her way, but on receiving a curt gesture to proceed with things, he opened up his leather folder. "Lord Woodbridge, I have reviewed the proposal drafted by Mr. Perkins, and though there may be one or two minor points that I must discuss further with my client, I believe we are willing to cooperate fully with you—"

A low snort that seemed to emanate from Aurora's general vicinity cut him off, but as she made no other sound, he cleared his throat and continued.

"Now, the legal grounds for annulment are, er, rather specific. Neither party is claiming that his lordship is . . . incapable of performing his marital duties—"

This time there was no mistaking the source of the interruption. "No doubt there would be entirely too many of his close female acquaintances willing to step forward and testify to the contrary," muttered Aurora under her breath, her eyes narrowing but still refusing to meet his.

Alex refrained from reaching out to throttle her.

Both Perkins and Seymour made a good deal of noise shuffling papers before the other man went on. "So, we have several options. We have discovered that one of His Lordship's names was omitted from the marriage license. This seems a less, er, objectionable way to proceed, rather than claiming that the marriage has not been . . . consummated." He paused, then looked up, his features pinched with embarrassment. "Of course, there will have to be the, or, normal sort of examination—"

"Perhaps we should consider changing the grounds for this proceeding," interrupted Aurora once more, this time with a deceptively sweet smile. "Instead of asking for an annulment, His Lordship could always sue the courts for a divorce. On the grounds of adul—"

"Gentlemen!" Alex's hand slammed down upon the table with a resounding bang. "If you don't mind, I wish to have a few words in private with my . . . wife."

"That will *not* be necessary, sir." To emphasize her point, Aurora took firm hold of Mr. Seymour's sleeve.

"In private," he repeated, his voice rising several decibels.

Perkins was already halfway to the door, the clerks right on his heels. Delayed by the need to extract his coat from Aurora's clenched fingers, Seymour took a fraction longer to bolt up out of his chair.

"Stop bellowing! It may intimidate these men but it has not the least effect on me, sir, as you well know." Aurora folded her arms across her chest. "And stop looking at me with that odious scowl," she added with a growl. "I find it particularly annoying when you make that face."

Alex found himself fighting to keep any semblance of composure. "What face? I am *not* making a face."

"Yes, you are. You do it whenever you decide to order people around. Your brows draw together like this, and then your left lip curls up just so." She mimicked his expression with frightening accuracy.

Both of the advisors stared at her with mouths agape.

His mouth quickly composed itself into a grim line. "Good Lord, must you always argue with me? Just once, will you try to act like a normal, biddable female and listen to reason?" he muttered.

"I thought you said the two of them were unacquainted," whispered Seymour.

"That was my understanding," replied Perkins, sounding equally perplexed.

"Well, they certainly sound like an old married couple. . . ."

"OUT!" The Earl of Woodbridge's command could best be described as a bellow. A very loud bellow.

The room was quickly emptied of all but the two of them.

Aurora stood up and moved over to stand by the high, mullioned windows. Her gaze drifted to the teeming street below for several moments before turning back to him. "*Well?* Now what?"

Alex drew in a deep breath. Lord, he had thought facing a troop of howling Kashmiri bandits required a steady nerve! *Ha!* He would much rather face off against a hundred flashing knives than the pair of emerald eyes that was now throwing daggered looks at his person. His teeth clamped together as he sought for a strategy to break the tense silence. He'd be damned if he would let her take the offensive, for it wasn't as if she didn't have a good deal to answer for herself.

"First of all, I suppose we had best deal with the matter at hand before anything else," he began haltingly. "It appears that we may have to revise the proposal my man of affairs presented to you in his letter, now that certain facts have come to light. Obviously we cannot proceed as before, due to the truth of—"

"Oh, we certainly wouldn't want to *lie*," she interrupted with withering sarcasm. "Would we, *Major Woodmore?* But really, what is yet one more untruth, when added to all the others?"

Alex flushed despite himself. "On a clandestine mission one never reveals one's real name," he muttered a bit defensively. "Other than that, I did not seek to—" His words cut off as he quickly recovered his equilibrium. "My God, you don't think I set out to *deliberately* deceive you, *Mrs. Sprague.*"

Two spots of color came to her cheeks. "Sprague was my grandmother's name, and considering all that had taken place, the only one I felt proud to bear. Anyway, I-I never thought of Fenimore as my real name. And it would have raised too many awkward questions when Robbie and I chose to leave my father's house and make our own way in the world."

He muttered something unintelligible under his breath. "Why was it you never took up residence at Rexford?"

"You need ask?" she replied in a scathing tone. "I was heartily sick of bullying male despots. Why should I have merely exchanged one for another?"

His color deepened, but he let the matter drop. "That is something we shall discuss at a later time, but for now, we had best address the current situation. What . . . happened in Scotland has made things a good deal more complicated—"

"Why?" Her chin came up. "If you insist on being a stickler for honesty, why not simply do as I have suggested and change the petition to one of divorce on the grounds of adultery. A physical examination, as Mr. Seymour so delicately put it, would confirm the fact."

"No! I will not permit it."

"Afraid you will become a laughingstock if it is bandied about that your wife was not satisfied with your own prowess, considerable though it may be?"

"There will be no sordid talk of adultery," he said through gritted teeth. "For your sake, not mine."

Aurora's lip curled in contempt. "Well, it *is* the truth, in thought if not in deed! I certainly did not know I was slipping between the sheets with my lawfully wedded husband!"

"The devil take it!" Alex was on his feet, too, and stalked to within arm's length of her. "Don't be such a stubborn fool, Aurora. Have you no idea what disgrace you would bring upon yourself and your friend Robbie with such an outrageous announcement? I would have no trouble weathering the scandal, but you should find yourself a total outcast from society."

She gave a harsh laugh. "As if it would matter! It isn't as if I have any desire to seek out another husband. Hell will freeze over before I should ever contemplate another marriage, especially with a so-called gentleman."

Alex knew full well that he deserved a measure of scorn for the past, but still he was cut by the razored disdain of her words. Without stopping to consider what he was saying, he lashed back. "You may sneer all you like at men in general and me in particular, but it was not ice flowing in your veins when you lay in my arms. Don't deny you took a full measure of enjoyment from the experience." His eyes flashed with a sudden glittering intensity. "It was high time someone broke through that prudish wall of your enforced maidenhood and showed you that you are capable of a passion other than anger."

Aurora turned white, and her hands clenched into fists. "You appear to have inherited not only a lofty title, sir, but the same arrogant, bullying attitudes of your despicable father. And mine. To think I ever thought you any different from the rest of them! A plague on *all* of you men who think females want or need nothing more than a tumble in bed to keep them satisfied and submissive." Her head jerked around so that her profile was in the shadows. "You may write up the papers however you wish. I shall inform Mr. Seymour I will sign *any* agreement to be rid of a cad like you."

With that, she turned on her heel and quit the room, the door slamming shut with a thunderous bang.

Chapter Eleven

Aurora stumbled into the cab of the waiting carriage, ignoring the offer of assistance from the startled footman standing by the steps. It was not until the door was latched shut and the horses began to move that she allowed the tears that had been welling in her eyes to fall.

This was absurd! she thought with a watery sniff. Had the plot unfolded on the pages of one of Robbie's horrid novels, she would have laughed herself silly, dismissing the author as guilty of possessing either an overly vivid imagination or an inclination toward the brandy bottle. Perhaps both, for on second thought, she would have considered it impossible that any sane person could have contrived such a story unless under the influence of strong spirits. Or drugs.

Indeed, she had felt as addled as an opium addict on hearing the distinct baritone voice behind her. Her first thought had been that she was hallucinating. Her second thought had been that she was going mad. Her third thought had been that if any solid object, such as a vase or marble bust, had

been close at hand, the Earl of Woodbridge would have a
rather large lump on his head.

Drat the man! How dare Alex Woodmore—or Fenimore
or Woodbridge or whatever his deuced name really was—
appear back in her life, just when her heart was beginning to
recover from the bruising of his lies. He *had* lied, in spirit,
if not in word, and somehow that had made the betrayal
seem even worse. She had allowed herself to be seduced by
the thought that Alex might have cared for her, when in truth
their liaison had been just another casual flirtation for him.
It had been the frisson of danger that had heated his blood,
not her in particular, and his admission after their lovemaking had merely been a none too subtle reminder that their
time together was at an end. He would move on to another
mission. And another mistress.

A righteous anger helped stem the tide of emotion flowing down her cheeks. She would never have fallen in . . .
bed with him had she known he was no better than all the
other philanderers the Sprague Agency for Distressed Females were used to investigating. And how dare he imply
that the unfortunate interlude in Scotland should have the
least effect on the original offer that he had made to his nominal wife. A deal was a deal. This was purely business, and
she wasn't about to let yet another quirk of male pride wreak
havoc with her life.

Somehow or another, this charade of a marriage was
going to be put to an end. And she, for once, was going to
reap some reward for having uttered those vows such a long,
long time ago.

Aurora gave another sniff and stared out the small window at the bustling scene on Bond Street. An assortment of
smart carriages and phaetons vied to squeeze past the drays
and wagons, while on either side of the cobbled way richly
dressed ladies and natty gentlemen strolled past ornate shop
fronts. She supposed she should have been captivated by all

the new sights and sounds before her, but in truth it was impossible to dwell on aught but an entirely different picture.

His raven locks, though still long, had been neatly trimmed, and his cheeks were smoothly shaven rather than covered with a rough stubble. Fine linen and tailored melton had replaced the rough garments of a nondescript laborer and an intricately knotted cravat covered the spot where once an intriguing bit of dark curls had peeked through his open shirt.

She sought to stifle a sigh. The first notes of his deep baritone voice had caused her insides to melt, and for an instant it had been not anger and hurt that had quickened her pulse but rather joy and . . . desire. Lord, she had wanted nothing so much as to fling herself into his arms and feel the reassuring warmth of his broad chest, the firm strength of his muscled shoulders. . . .

The hardening of her mouth turned the sigh into more of a snort.

It was true that Alex was a very attractive man. But he was also a lout and a liar. And a practiced lecher, she reminded herself with some heat. The skill of his kisses and his intimate caresses made it quite clear that he had a good deal of experience in more than the art of warfare. She blinked on recalling a certain book among his things. Tactics and training, indeed! The major was well schooled in storming the strongest of defenses. And obviously well used to coming out on top.

Wretched man! Using such sentiment like a piece of ice to cool the heat flaring up in her very core, Aurora flung herself back against the squabs. She would cease to think about the sensuous curve of his lips and the strong line of his jaw. Nor would she dwell on how his sapphire eyes sparkled with the rich intensity of two precious jewels, for in reality they were only paste, a mocking imitation of something of real value. Just like the rest of him.

By the time the carriage rolled to a stop in front of the town house on Half Moon Street, it was no longer the trace of tears that marred her countenance but a ferocious scowl.

"Oh dear," ventured Miss Robertson, on looking up from the book she was reading as Aurora stalked into the cozy sitting room. "I take it that one or two complications arose during the meeting?"

"Complications?" Aurora threw her reticule down onto the nearest chair, resulting in the muffled sound of breaking glass. "That, my dear Robbie, could be the understatement of the century."

The bang of the door still reverberated in his ears as Alex regarded the waxed panels with a mixture of anger and exasperation. She was right. His last statement had hardly been a very gentlemanly—or a very wise—thing to say, given what he knew to be her sentiments on the relationship between men and women.

It had been cruel to speak as if what had taken place between them had been purely physical. Though he had yet to unravel the tangle of her emotions, he sensed that she had suffered a loss of more than her maidenhood that fateful night. The fact that she had fled without so much as confronting him was a mark of how deeply she must have been hurt. There were not many situations, he mused with a flicker of a smile, that would put Aurora Sprague—or rather Fenimore—to flight. Had she been frightened as well as wounded? But why?

Hell's teeth! It was not as if she had been less secretive and tight-lipped about her past than he had been. She had no right to accuse him of subterfuge when she was as guilty of disguising the truth as he was.

Still, he should have tempered his cynical response. However, the truth of the matter was that he had not exactly

been thinking clearly. Indeed, he had not been thinking at
all, for his brain had suddenly refused to function properly
the moment she had first turned around.

It still wasn't.

Aurora was his wife.

Surely he was dreaming! Or foxed. Or insane. His hand
raked through his locks, as if searching for some other plau-
sible explanation. But no, fingers scraping scalp forced him
to admit he was unfortunately awake, and unfortunately
sober. His sanity, however, was still in question.

A timid knock came from the other side of the polished
oak. His gruff reply caused it to open a fraction, allowing a
pair of anxious eyes to peer in.

"My lord . . ."

With a harried sigh, he motioned for Perkins to enter.

"Er, L-Lady Woodbridge insisted on signing the papers,
saying that should you wish to amend any of the first pages,
she, er, had no objections." He cleared his throat with some
nervousness. "You made quite clear that you wished to settle this matter as quickly as possible. Shall Seymour and I
see that the relevant parts are revised and petition filed
today?"

Alex stared at the sheaf of documents in the other man's
hands. "Leave them with me."

"But, sir—"

"I said, *leave them.*"

A certain young lady might be impervious to his tone of
command, but it seemed to have the desired effect on others.
The papers immediately dropped to the table with a thud.
"Yes, my lord!"

Alex was still looking at them a short while later as they
lay beside him on the seat of his carriage. Wrapped neatly
within a binder of leather, they looked to have been shuffled,
squared, and put well in order. He wished he might say the

same for his thoughts. His mind felt as jolted and jostled as
the wooden wheels flying over the cobblestones.

Aurora was his wife! he repeated again, though the words
still seemed as incomprehensible as a passage of Sanskrit.

Contemplating the almost farcical turn things had taken
only caused his brooding mood to grow worse. By the time
his butler threw open the front door of his imposing town
house he was in the blackest of humors, and his polished
Hessians beat an angry tattoo down the checkered marble
floor as he stomped to his study. The package containing the
annulment papers was tossed on his desk, and with a dark
scowl, he took a cheroot from his humidor and struck up a
light. Then, as a plume of smoke rose up toward the painted
ceiling, he paused for an instant, catching sight of his reflection in the gilt mirror over the mantel.

He wiggled his brows. The left corner of his lip moved
up and down.

Ridiculous! He did *not* make a face, odious or otherwise.

Another series of wafting rings drifted through the air.
Damnation, he fumed, drawing so hard on the tightly rolled
tobacco that the tip glowed a fiery orange. He had every
right to be burning with anger. Any husband would be in a
foul temper on discovering that the female who, above all
others, was supposed to accord him unquestioning respect
was obstinate, willful, disobedient, and possessed of a
tongue like a saber.

Not to mention having a mind of her own that was just as
sharply honed. How dare she refuse the protection of his
name, however meager the benefits had been! How dare she
risk her neck—and name—in dangerous exploits! How dare
she make it so plain that the notion of him as her husband
was a horrible one.

Alex swore again and began pacing before the banked
fire. Aurora had entirely too many radical notions to make a
proper, biddable wife. He should be delighted with the no-

tion of ending the marriage now that he knew to whom he was leg-shackled!

Hmmph! With a grunt of satisfaction, he tossed the half-finished cheroot into the hearth and took a seat at his desk. His eyes fell once again upon the legal documents. The sooner they were filed, the sooner he would be free to choose a docile, well-mannered young lady from among the cream of the *ton* to be his countess. Someone who would not dream of voicing her own opinion or contradicting his orders.

The package was shifted to the corner of the desk. He would deliver them back to Perkins once he had a chance to make a few final adjustments to the details of the monetary settlements. But first, there were a number of other pressing matters that needed the new earl's attention.

For the next several hours Alex forced himself to pore over a sheaf of papers concerning his various estates and investments. Finally, he threw down his pen in frustration, realizing that he hadn't been paying the least heed to what he had been reading. *What the devil was wrong with him?* On countless nights, in countless dreary surroundings, he had fallen asleep dreaming of what it would be like to have a real home of his own. Now fate had dealt him a lucky hand and he should be chafing at the bit to make the most of it. Much as he had pretended otherwise over the years, he cared deeply for his ancestral lands and looked forward to the challenge of building a stable, meaningful life for himself.

So why was his mind wandering so far astray that it might well have still been in India?

The ledger in which he had been writing snapped shut. A glass or two of fine brandy would no doubt help settle the strange agitation affecting his thoughts. He rose and walked in the direction of the formal drawing room, his steps echoing through the deserted hallways. A lone maid peeked out of the music room, then ducked back inside. Two footmen carrying a settee out of the morning room scurried toward the back stairs, neither daring to venture a glance at the new earl. Trying to ignore the sense of malaise that continued to grip him, Alex picked up his pace, determined to loosen its hold with as much of the aged French spirits as was necessary.

Once he had poured a stiff drink, he sought to relax, but his eyes couldn't stop roaming around the ornate space, taking in the gilt chairs, the brocade sofas, the perfectly creased draperies, all of which looked to have been undisturbed for months, if not years. Lord, he hadn't realized that Woodbridge House was so . . . empty. Chillingly empty. With a stab of fierce longing, he found himself missing the warmth of companionship, the heat of a shared smile, the spark of soft laughter.

His gaze fell on the classical painting above the fireplace. It depicted the Goddess Diana in full hunting regalia. Bow at the ready, eyes alert, chin tilted in youthful confidence, she looked fearless and undaunted by the dangers that might be lurking in the woods around her. Alex stared at the lovely profile, struck by how the artist had captured both vulnerability and strength in the feminine features.

All at once, the glass of spirits shattered against the marble of the hearth.

Women!

He had never allowed any female to pierce the armor of his indifference with her arrows, but it seemed that all the recent upheavals in his life had caused a momentary chink in his defenses. Even so, he should have been far too experienced in dodging danger for the barb to have found its mark.

His teeth clenched at the sight of the amber liquid dripping down the veined marble. It wasn't as if any real blood had been spilled. The wound was no more than a mere prick, he assured himself. Why, he had only to repair to his club and the familiar camaraderie of fellow men for the discomfort of it to be quickly forgotten. The shuffle of cards and the savoring of a good claret would in no time banish any lingering rawness caused by thoughts of a certain young lady. Turning away from the shards of glass buried among the embers, Alex rang for his butler and gave orders for the carriage to be brought around. His hat and greatcoat soon appeared, along with his elegant gloves and walking stick. Within minutes he was off.

There was no discernible change in White's from ten years ago. He handed his things to a grizzled porter who had undoubtedly served his father, then made his way to one of the gaming rooms, fully intent on falling into an evening of deep play and equally deep cups. It was a blessed relief to see nothing but male faces, he thought on regarding the various tables. The gravelly tones and bawdy comments of the masculine voices sounded just as familiar here in Mayfair as they did in Bombay and Lisbon. It should prove a most satisfactory way to while away the hours until dawn.

A second glance around the room caused him to hesitate. For the most part, the crowd was made up of strangers. There were several men whom he vaguely recognized, but each of them was too engrossed in his own game and his own friends to notice the figure at the door. Alex shifted uncomfortably from foot to foot, strangely loath to approach any of the groups. In glum silence, he listened to the soft slap of cards, the rattle of dice, and the murmured exchanges of triumph and disgust.

"I say, Woodbridge, is it?" A gentleman seated at the nearest gaming table looked up as one of his companions shuffled the deck in preparation for dealing a new hand.

Alex nodded, trying to match the beaked nose and wavy blond hair combed straight back from a high forehead with an actual name.

"Thought I'd got it right. Heard Ainslie greet you the other day as you were leaving Weston's. Newly arrived from the Peninsula to take up the title, eh? Word has it you have seen action in all manner of exotic locales during your years away from English soil."

A ghost of a smile played on Alex's lips. "It appears you are remarkably well informed, sir."

"Surely you haven't forgotten how quickly every bit of gossip and all the latest *on dits* make the rounds about Town," replied the other man with a hearty laugh. He gave a wave of his hand. "Come, join us. I'm Uxton." His gesture swept to the others gathered around the green baize. "And this is Foxcroft, Hartsleigh, Cresthill, and Grenville."

They all exchanged polite nods as room was made for another chair. Alex sat down, telling himself he should feel quite gratified that things were going according to his plan. He would soon be trading jovial banter and gibes with new friends, and listening with detached amusement to good-natured asides about other members of the *ton*. Several bottles of claret were ordered and he settled in to enjoy his companions and a long night of play.

Their conversation soon caused his spirits to plummet. The observations were shallow, the comments vacuous. They appeared interested primarily in chipping away at the reputation of others in order to build up their own stature, rather than engage in any meaningful talk. All at once he found himself wishing he could hear Aurora's assessment of the present company. It was her sage judgment and forthright opinion that he valued above all others. He knew all too well how her sharp insight would cut right through the pompous pretension and self-important smugness he could see firmly entrenched on the five faces circling the table.

Damnation! It made no sense at all. He was furious with her, and yet he missed the sound of her voice, no matter that the words were more often than not saying something outrageous. More than that, he had to admit that what he really missed was the feel of her slender fingers entwined with his. Her touch was what would help soothe the cursed chill of loneliness from his bones.

The contents of his glass disappeared in one swallow, and with it went all desire to remain where he was. Somehow the idea of gaming and drinking no longer held any appeal when it was Aurora's face he saw on every card and the memory of her sweet embraces that had him growing more intoxicated by the moment . . .

His chair pushed back abruptly. "I'm afraid you gentlemen will have to excuse me." Ignoring the startled looks from all around, he folded his hand and stood up. "I must be off."

"Deucedly odd behavior," muttered one of the players as Alex retreated toward the front hall. "Must come from spending so much time away from civilization."

Odd did not begin to describe the way he was feeling. Nothing was making any sense! If a warm caress was what he needed to chase away his dark mood, why the devil was he mooning over Aurora, who now held him in nothing but contempt? He was very angry with her, too, and well within his rights to feel such sentiments.

Enough of the plaguey female! If intimate companionship was what he needed, then he would seek it out now. There were plenty of other willing women who possessed more beauty, more charm, and certainly more knowledge of how to give pleasure to a man. A few words were exchanged with the porter, along with a coin or two, and the address of the most exclusive madam in Town was passed along.

The coach rolled to a halt in front of a small but elegant town house tucked away on a small side street of the fashionable neighborhood. A sliver of honeyed light shone from a small gap in discreetly drawn red velvet draperies at the front windows. It cast a warm glow over the white marble stairs leading up to the door, beckoning with the sensuous promise of sultry delights hidden within.

His boot was halfway to the ground when suddenly he yanked it back with a scathing oath directed at his own head. The door slammed shut and, still muttering under his breath, he rapped on the trap and ordered the confused coachman to spring the horses for home.

Giving up all pretense of trying to sort out his tangled emotions, Alex dismissed his valet and stripped off his finely tailored clothes, letting them fall in a heap on the thick carpet. Not bothering with a nightshirt, he slipped between the sheets of his large tester bed. A very large and very lonely bed. Tucking one of the eiderdown pillows under an arm, he turned on his side and closed his eyes. A number of minutes passed before he stirred and tugged the covers over his chin. Then he tossed. And turned again, willing sleep to come.

But despite all his efforts to the contrary, deep, dreamless oblivion proved elusive. Not so were haunting thoughts of . . . his wife. He rolled onto his back and let out a muffled groan, imagining the feel of her skin, the texture of her hair, the sweetness of her lips, and the innocent rapture of her response to his lovemaking. He swore, but he could not banish the image of her molten green eyes or the endearing tilt of her chin when she was roused to anger. Slowly but surely, the anger within his own breast burned down to a flicker of remorse.

Perhaps he was more to blame for what had happened that afternoon than he had admitted. His hasty words had been what caused tempers to flare and cutting insults to be exchanged. So it was only right that he should consider apologizing for the breach in behavior. It was what honor demanded, he assured himself, and not because it would afford him another chance to meet with her.

On further thought, there seemed to be no reason they could not, as rational adults, both agree to be civil to each other until things were settled. After all, it would soon be over and then they would both be free to do as they pleased. In the meantime . . .

It suddenly occurred to him that Aurora and her companion had never been to London before. He could at least make an attempt to behave like a true gentleman by offering to show them the sights while they were here.

Chapter Twelve

Miss Robertson regarded the impeccably tailored coat and the starched perfection of the cravat over the rims of her spectacles for several long moments before her gaze slid down to the fitted fawn breeches and polished Hessians. "Hmmph," she sniffed. "It appears that your legs, at least, are a good deal steadier this morning than they were ten years ago, sir." In a lower voice she added, "I wonder whether the same can be said for your character."

Alex repressed a twitch of his lips. "You are, I take it, the infamous Robbie. I hope I shall not come to regret the fact that it was not you who ended up sunk in the waters off Ayr."

The former governess's mouth dropped in momentary shock before it resumed its pursed scowl.

"An attempt at humor," he murmured. "Perhaps it is still a bit early in the day for such things."

If anything, the scowl deepened.

He cleared his throat. "Er, would you kindly inform . . . my wife that I wish a few words with her."

"No."

His brow rose a touch. "No?"

"No." Miss Robertson crossed her arms. "Since it is rumored that you attended Oxford, I trust that the meaning of the word is quite clear."

Alex took a step closer and fixed her with a grim smile. "No. It is not. It has been a long time since I was required to study the nuances of language, so in this particular instance, perhaps you will humor me with a more precise definition."

She swallowed hard but refused to back down. "Very well, sir. *No,* I won't inform her, because *no*, she doesn't want to speak to you."

"You are sure?"

"Yes."

His lips twitched. "Perhaps you would care to give a detailed definition of the word 'yes.' . . ."

Before another round of verbal sparring could begin, the door to the morning room opened, framing Aurora in a halo of sunlight. "I appreciate your concern, Robbie, but I'm capable of fighting my own battles." She fixed Alex with an icy look, hoping it would mask the frisson of happiness she felt run through her on seeing him again. "Besides, I think we may trust that his lordship is not intent on causing anyone bodily harm this morning." There was a deliberate pause before she added a muttered aside. "I won't promise that the same can be said for me."

He made a polite bow. "As I am not unused to danger, madam, I am willing to take the risk."

She turned slightly and motioned for him to enter the room. Miss Robertson made to follow, but the door was quietly, yet firmly, drawn shut. Aurora moved to a spot by the window, placing a small japanned settee between them, and began to toy with a Staffordshire figurine that sat on the matching side table.

"Choosing a weapon already?" he murmured dryly.

She kept her eyes averted so she didn't have to see how the snug cut of his coat set off the muscled breadth of his shoulders, or how the stripe of his slubbed-silk waistcoat picked up the exact shade of his eyes. "I assume you would prefer a truce for the moment."

"I was going to suggest something of the sort."

Her fingers tightened on the smooth curves of fired clay. "Why? That is, why exactly are you here, sir?"

Alex made as if to speak, but stopped as his eyes traveled from the narrow silk sash of her stylish day dress to the rucked bodice, which revealed a good deal more creamy skin than her former gowns were wont to show. He cleared his throat, letting his gaze drift up to the loose knot of curls that her new lady's maid had arranged to graze against one shoulder. "You know, with all the, er, distractions of yesterday, I neglected to mention how . . . well you look."

The figurine fell to the thick Axminster carpet.

"I was . . . worried about you," he continued in a low voice. "Even now, I have a Runner out searching for you, to ensure that you made it safely to wherever it is you call home."

Her gaze flew up to meet his. "But you needn't have troubled. I-I told you on more than several occasions that I was quite used to taking care of myself."

"Yes. So you did."

Confused by the rawness in his voice, Aurora looked away again. "I must also remark that you clean up rather nicely, Major Woodmore," she said after an awkward moment of silence, hoping that a note of dry humor might serve to ease the tension that had crept into both of their words.

The comment did indeed evoke a twitch of his lips. "As my talents at washing linen or stropping a razor are, as you know, rather rudimentary, it does make a difference to have a skilled laundress and valet at one's service."

"Ah, the advantages of being an earl." Lord, how she had missed their easy banter! She bent down to retrieve what she had dropped in order to hide the spasm of longing that suddenly twisted her features. "But I imagine you did not come here to discuss sartorial matters, my lord."

"No." Alex clasped his hands behind his back. "I came to apologize for what I said yesterday," he said in a halting voice. "The situation took me by surprise, to say the least, and I'm afraid that the shock of it caused me to let fly with some words that, well, that I wish I might recall. I didn't mean them as they sounded."

"My own conduct was far from exemplary, sir. I fear my temper also got the better of me, and I uttered a number of things that were . . . unfair." She drew in a deep breath as she shoved the small figurine into her pocket. "Considering all things, perhaps we may both be excused for a certain lapse in judgment."

He studied the tilt of her profile, a thoughtful expression spreading over his lean features. "Yes, I couldn't agree more."

Aurora forced a cheerful face. She imagined that, apologies made, he meant to take himself off, maybe for good. The prospect of never seeing his face again should have her feeling not merely cheerful, but ecstatic. "Good!" she said in a voice so brittle she feared it might break. "We have that settled, so you need not give us another thought, sir. Now that the papers are signed, Robbie and I can go home. And you can go about doing . . . whatever it is that titled lords do in Town."

A look of faint amusement flashed in his eyes. "As I am rather new to the job, I have not the slightest idea what those things are."

"Oh." Her lips pursed. "Well, given the broad range of

your other skills, I am sure you will pick up the knack of it very quickly."

He gave a little cough. "Actually there is something else I wish to discuss." His gaze strayed to the plump sofa facing two claw-footed wing chairs. "Might we sit down?"

The color rose to her cheeks on realizing how sadly lacking in drawing-room manners she had shown herself to be. It would serve her right if he thought her nothing more than a churlish country hoyden. "Of course," she said through gritted teeth, reminding herself that his opinion of her mattered not a whit.

Aurora sat down on the sofa and with what she hoped was a graceful wave of her hand indicated he should take the facing chair. To her dismay, he ignored the gesture and took a seat close by her side. So close that his thigh threatened to crush the folds of her skirts. Somehow the nearness of his person, despite the layers of cloth between them, was making her skin feel even warmer. She essayed a deep breath to steady her nerves, but that proved a big mistake. The scent of bay rum and woodsy herbs, coupled with an unmistakable undertone of Alex himself, filled her lungs. The effect on her senses was like that of a bottle of brandy being downed in one hurried gulp. The sofa seemed to be listing heavily to the left, and she felt herself sliding slowly toward the intricate knot of his cravat.

"A pleasant spot, is it not?"

"What?" she gasped, finding that the notion of her nose coming to rest with an ignominious thud against his linen was not a pleasant one at all. Determined not to make a complete cake of herself, she managed to regain a measure of control and remain upright. With a small flounce, she threw her shoulders back against the damask cushions, as if she had merely been seeking a more comfortable position.

"The room," he replied mildly. "I have always thought

Aunt Letitia's morning room to be an extremely cheery place, especially when the sun comes through the windows just so."

Aurora eyed him warily. His arm had been thrown negligently along the carved back of the sofa so that his hand was nearly brushing the nape of her neck. *Drat the man!* How could he sit there looking so utterly composed when all she could think about was how much she longed for those long, lithe fingers to skim a light caress over the exposed skin and then entwine themselves in the very depth of her curls?

A series of little shivers shuddered up and down her spine, and to cover up she was forced to jab at one of the cushions with her elbow.

"Is something causing you discomfort?" Alex asked blandly. "I should be happy to fetch an extra pillow?"

"No need," she muttered. Resolved to match his cool composure, she affected a look of studied indifference and brushed at a minute wrinkle on her sleeve. "Just a small lump, but it's taken care of." Her hands rearranged themselves primly on her lap. "If you don't mind, sir," she said briskly, "perhaps we could get on with it—you said you had another matter to discuss."

"Hmm. Yes, I did." It seemed, however, that he was in no hurry to speak. He crossed his leg, shifting his thigh ever closer to hers.

She crabbed sideways several inches. "Well?"

"My, my, getting right down to business, I see," he murmured.

Her face scrunched into an odd grimace. "Why else would we be sitting here talking with each other?"

He looked at her with an equally odd expression. "Why else, indeed."

She thought she finally detected a hint of emotion beneath the show of sangfroid as his fingers moved away from their position by her ear to give a nervous tug at the corner of his waistcoat. Her suspicion was further confirmed by what looked to be a slight tensing in the muscle of his jaw.

Ha! So the Earl of Woodbridge was not quite as at ease as he wished to appear either.

Alex seemed to be inspecting the polished tips of his boots. "Very well. I was going to suggest that, given we are both adults with a modicum of intelligence and common sense, we might agree to act in a rational, civilized manner in each other's presence."

"You are, in other words, suggesting that we don't go at each other like cats and dogs."

He gave a nod.

"That seems to be assuming we are going to be having some sort of contact in the future." Her brows came together. "I thought everything had been settled. The papers have been signed, and as I told your man of affairs, you may make any changes you wish to the exact wording. From what Mr. Seymour said, there is no reason—"

"There may be one or two, ah, minor details that still have to be attended to. The solicitors may require us to meet again, and the atmosphere might be more conducive to reaching a mutually acceptable resolution if there were not the threat of flying inkwells. Or reticules."

"I-I suppose that makes some sense," she mused.

"I thought I could count on your practical bent of mind to see the advantages of such an agreement. In the meantime, it would be advisable for you not to leave London until everything is settled once and for all." He reached down to flick an invisible speck from the mirrorlike leather. "As it is impossible to predict just how long that will be, I thought that perhaps you and Miss Robertson would care to see some of the sights the city has to offer. I believe I remember you mentioning that neither of you had ever been here before."

"You are offering to squire us around Town?"

"The acrobats at Astley's Amphitheatre, Mrs. Siddons at Haymarket, the menagerie at the Tower, the fireworks at Vauxhall Gardens. That sort of thing." He gave a low cough. "Polite Society deems it a tad more acceptable if females, especially ones new to the *ton,* are accompanied by a male escort when they go out. I don't believe you know anyone else in London."

Aurora chewed on her lower lip. "Robbie would adore the chance to visit all the places she has read about."

"The ices at Gunther's are also said to be delectable," he murmured.

"I-I shall think about it."

"Do."

It would mean spending a good deal of time in Alex's company, she reflected. Sitting with him in the theater, close enough to breathe in the subtle scent of his musky cologne. Strolling down a torchlit path, her arm resting on his sleeve. Conversing during the carriage rides, forced to watch every nuance of expression that played on the molded curves of his lips.

Aurora set her jaw and turned slightly. "On further consideration, I don't believe your services will be necessary, my lord." The words came out rather more sharply than she intended.

His expression remained neutral, but the color of his eyes clouded to a stormy shade of blue. "May I ask why?"

"Don't you see, sir, how it would all be very confusing? Not to speak of creating a good deal of gossip that would surely cause you embarrassment when the time comes to seek a real wife." Her chin rose a fraction. "I mean, we can hardly appear as a married couple on . . . intimate terms, then announce an annulment, without giving rise to all sorts of awkward speculation."

"If that is your only concern, you needn't fret overly on

it. Since some story was needed to explain your presence in my great-aunt's town house, I have already seen to it that she has written to several of her friends who can't resist a bit of gossip. By now, all the *ton* will know that you are Mrs. Sprague, a family connection from the country who has been invited to make use of her town house while she is away. I would be seen as merely doing my duty by escorting you and your companion around Town," he answered quietly.

"You appear to have given this some thought, sir."

"Why not discuss it with Miss Robertson?" He rose and walked to the bank of high Palladian windows where the sunlight silhouetted his chiseled profile. "Have you had a chance to drive through Hyde Park?" he asked abruptly.

"No." There was a wistful note to the syllable. "Not yet."

"I shall bring my carriage around at five, when all of fashionable Society comes out for the grand promenade." Aurora made to speak, but he went on too quickly to allow an interruption. "You and your friend should at least see such a grand sight while you are here. As for the rest, well, you may tell me your final decision at that time." He gave a hurried bow and left the room before she could think of any reply.

"We are invited for a drive in Hyde Park? Past the Serpentine? Down Rotten Row? At the height of the Season, when the cream of the *ton* will be on parade?" An expression of delight slowly split Miss Robertson's broad features as the import of the words sunk in. "Oh, what fun!"

"What fun, indeed," muttered Aurora through gritted teeth.

The older woman put down her teacup and fixed her former charge with a searching look. After some moments she brushed a wisp of gray hair away from the bridge of her spectacles. "My dear, you needn't do this for my sake. If the prospect of riding out with the earl is repugnant to you, we shall of course not even consider it." Her lips pursed in a wry smile. "Since I have managed to exist for over fifty-five years without seeing the Tulips of the *ton* canter through the park or the young bucks ogle the actresses treading the boards, I imagine I shall not go into a state of permanent decline if the opportunity does not present itself now."

Aurora crumbled the rest of her scone between her fingers. "Don't be silly. I know how much you would enjoy it and I should be a selfish beast were I to deny you the pleasure of it." She exhaled deeply. "After all, I lived with the dratted man for more than a—" Her voice cut off sharply as her face turned a vivid shade of crimson. "Er, that did not come out exactly as I meant it."

Miss Robertson ducked her head to hide a grin. "Ah, well, that finally answers that."

"That answers *what?"*

The former governess deliberately took her time in buttering a piece of toast and applying a dollop of strawberry preserves. "You have been a bit vague about what, exactly, happened between you and the dashing major during your little adventure. But now, things have become a trifle clearer since this morning."

"What do you mean?" Aurora's voice sounded as if a large hand were around her throat and squeezing very hard.

"For one thing, I saw the way you looked at the man. And the way he looked at you."

"Ha! Both of us were no doubt looking at each other as if we were contemplating murder," she muttered, keeping her eyes studiously averted from the keen gaze of her companion.

Miss Robertson slowly brushed a crumb from her chin with a pat of the thick damask napkin. "Ha! The crime of passion you looked to be contemplating was most definitely not murder." The last morsel went into her mouth and she took her time in swallowing it. "Not that what you were thinking of was by any means a crime, mind you. The two of you are, after all, married."

Aurora made a choking sound.

"There is just one other question I would like to ask, if you don't mind, my dear."

The choking ceased, replaced by utter silence.

"Is falling in love at all like it is described in the horrid novels?"

Her mouth fell agape. For several moments it hung slack; then its movement began to resemble the actions of a fish out of water. Finally, a strangled squeak made its way out. "Robbie! You don't really think for one instant that I am in l-l-love with the Earl of Woodbridge!"

"Well, I know that among the *ton* it is not considered very fashionable to have a *tendre* for one's husband, but there are exceptions—"

"I do *not* have a *tendre* for that odious, arrogant, insufferable, overbearing, ill-tempered . . ." She paused, sputtering, as if groping for more words.

"If you are searching for additional adjectives, you forgot 'devilishly handsome,' and 'wittily amusing,'" murmured Miss Robertson with an air of great innocence. "Though it does not maintain the same grammatical style."

"Robbie!"

"You're right, it's not quite the appropriate time for an English lesson. I can see that at the present moment you are in no mood to discuss the nuances of sentence structure," she went on airily. "So both subjects can certainly wait until another time. In any case, I wish to make a quick trip to the milliner on Bond Street to pick up your new bonnet, which will look quite dashing with your new carriage dress. Then I think I shall take a nap so that I am ready for when his lordship arrives." The napkin came up for a final pat at the older woman's mouth, its heavy folds hiding the look of unholy amusement tugging at its corners. "Good gracious, this stay in London is promising to become even more interesting than I imagined. I do hope my nerves will hold up to all the excitement."

Robbie's nerves seemed to be surviving the ordeal quite well, fumed Aurora some hours later. It was her own frayed temper she was worried about. A mild breeze ruffled the emerald ribbons of her new chipped-straw bonnet and caused a lock of hair to fall over her cheek. She brushed it back, trying hard to keep a scowl off her face.

"That is Lady Trenboro," murmured Alex to Miss Robertson. He then nodded a polite greeting to a buxom blonde of uncertain years who sported an unusual frogged jacket designed to accentuate her rather obvious assets. The bright canary yellow silk was matched to perfection by the color of the stylish phaeton that she drove herself. "She is considered to be a bit of an . . . eccentric," he added as her team of jet-black horses maneuvered through the crush of carriages.

"Isn't the word more like outrageous, my lord?" Miss Robertson gave a little snort. "From what I have gleaned from the newspapers, she is considered to have an appetite for men that rivals that of Catherine the Great. Aren't both Lord Atherton and Viscount Havlock rumored to be her latest paramours?"

Alex stifled a chuckle. "It seems you are particularly well read, Miss Robertson. What other subjects do you favor, besides history and, er, current events?"

"The works of Mrs. Radcliffe," muttered Aurora under her breath.

A mischievous twinkle came to his eyes. "You seem to have more than a passing interest in books, too, as I recall."

If one had been at hand, she thought, it would have landed smack between those two glittering sapphire orbs. "Actually, I tend to spend more of my time writing up my reports." She smiled sweetly at four turbaned matrons who were practically falling over each other in the back of their open landau in order to gain a peek at the new Earl of Woodbridge's companions. "On the subject of married men and their various lies and peccadilloes. But then, you no doubt recall that as well." That wiped the grin from his face rather quickly, she noted with some satisfaction as she settled back against the soft leather seat and watched two dandies on horseback vie for the attention of a fetching young lady walking with a dour-faced chaperon.

Miss Robertson made a reproving sound in the back of her throat. "Really, my dear, there is no need to snap at Alex—"

"*Alex!*" repeated Aurora in some amazement. This was outside of enough! No more than twenty minutes had passed and already the dratted man had charmed so formidable a female adversary as Robbie. She would have to keep a more careful eye on this whole charade lest things really get out of hand.

Two spots of color came to the older woman's wrinkled cheeks. "I-I—that is, Lord Woodbridge insisted that we mustn't rest on formalities if we are to present to Society that we are friends."

"We are *not* friends," grumbled Aurora. "We would all do well to remember that."

Alex appeared unperturbed by her waspish words. He nodded a greeting to the occupants of yet another carriage, then calmly pointed out a well-known general to Miss Robertson and launched into an amusing anecdote that had the other woman back smiling in a matter of moments.

Aurora's mood became even glummer. *This had definitely not been a good idea.* It was not only Robbie's reactions she was concerned about, but her own. There had been no denying that her pulse had quickened on seeing Alex descend from his carriage at the appointed hour, dressed in his elegant navy coat and snug, buff-colored breeches. She could only hope that he hadn't noticed any flutter of the draperies that would have revealed her clandestine observation. And even now she had to keep her face averted to hide the heated glow of her cheeks and the look of longing in her eyes.

Surely Robbie couldn't be right. She sucked in a bit of her lower lip. How hopelessly absurd! Surely she had not developed a real *tendre* for the man. And what did it matter if she had? she told herself roughly. The Earl of Woodbridge possessed no such tender feelings. What he possessed was a sheaf of neatly penned foolscap that would soon serve to sever any connection between them, romantic or otherwise.

Whether she wished it or not.

A peal of loud laughter rang out from a nearby carriage. Aurora was grateful for the sound since it covered what she feared had been a tiny sniffle.

Alex was just finishing his story when he remarked on the vehicle swinging in from the left. A whisper that sounded suspiciously close to an oath formed on his lips. "Good Lord, it is Lady Renfrew who is bearing down on us," he said in a slightly louder voice. "She is one of my Aunt Letitia's more outspoken cronies, so prepare yourselves, ladies, for—"

His warning was cut off by the sharp rap of a silvertipped cane against the lacquered panel of his vehicle.

"Alexander. Or Woodbridge, as I suppose I must now call you." It was, thought Aurora, nothing short of remarkable that such a deep-throated bellow could emerge from such a frail creature. "Hmmph! Hard to imagine the grubby-faced little rapscallion who smashed three of my drawing-room windows with his cricket ball is now an earl, but life has a way of turning out as one least expects it to. Take my word for it." Another rap of the cane punctuated her pronouncement. "You are still the very naughty boy I remember. Haven't paid me a visit yet, although I've heard you have been in Town for ages."

Alex murmured a handsome apology that appeared to mollify the elderly lady somewhat.

"Hmmph. Well, no doubt you have had numerous demands on your time, but I expect you will rectify the oversight in short order." Lady Renfrew paused to polish the lens of an ornate man's quizzing glass that hung around her neck on a silk ribbon. When raised to her eye, it gave her the look of a diminutive cyclops. "Your gallivanting across the globe seems to have done you no harm. Still a handsome devil, I see." The glass then focused on the other occupants of the earl's carriage. "Hmmph. What's this I hear about relatives staying at Letitia's town house?" The cane gave another whack to the side of the carriage. "She mentioned nothing of the sort to me."

"Must have slipped her mind." Alex gave a winning smile. "Unlike you, dear Lady Cassandra, her wits are not quite as sharp as they used to be."

Lady Renfrew gave a low snort, but the corners of her mouth turned up. She surveyed Miss Robertson before letting the lens linger on Aurora. "Unusual gel," she remarked after some moments. The one magnified eye narrowed. "Are you on the marriage mart?" she demanded with unabashed interest.

"No!" Taken rather aback by the question, Alex's brows drew together. *"Mrs.* Sprague is not—"

Aurora fixed him with an odd stare, then turned to Lady Renfrew with a sweet smile and interrupted his halting reply. "What Lord Woodbridge means is 'not exactly.' I am a missus, but I have . . . lost my husband."

The elderly lady gave a knowing nod. "Well, there's

some who vastly prefer a gel with some experience to one fresh from the schoolroom. It seems you also have some spirit as well, which may or may not be in your favor. Have you an inheritance?"

"None to speak of."

"Hmmph. That will make things more difficult." She slanted a sideways glance at Alex. "Perhaps Woodbridge may be convinced to cough up some blunt. You are a relation, after all."

Aurora dropped her lashes. "While the earl has kindly given some attention to certain aspects of my finances, I must confess it had not occurred to me to discuss the matter of a dowry."

"Don't be shy, gel! A lady must take matters into her own hands at times, if she wishes to succeed in this world."

"Lord, as if she needs to be reminded," muttered Alex under his breath.

Lady Renfrew shot him a keen look that showed her ears to be in as good form as her lungs. "I imagine Woodbridge will do what is right. He was always the best of the plaguey lot of Fenimores, even if he was a handful at times." She let the quizzing glass fall back to her wizened chest. "Bring her with you when you visit, Alexander. She appears to be more interesting than most milk-and-water misses." With that the cane came down once more, this time against the panel of her own door. The driver, apparently well used to his employer's little quirks, immediately started the horses off at a smart trot.

Alex turned to Aurora as soon as Lady Renfrew's vehicle had moved off, the irritation writ plain on his face. "What the devil made you say such a farradiddle such as—"

Although the poke of her bonnet hid her expression, the tilt of her chin was clear enough indication of her refusal to be cowed by his tone. "What do you mean, sir? What I said is the truth, is it not?"

His mouth thinned into a grim line, but he made no answer. After a few moments of awkward silence, he shifted in his seat and fell back to regaling Miss Robertson with more pithy commentary on the various personages who were making their way along Rotten Row.

Aurora jerked her head around to look out over the crowd of strangers on her side of the park, suddenly feeling rather sick to her stomach. It *was* the truth, she told herself. So why was the taste of it so bitter?

She choked down a groan. Perhaps it was no longer possible to avoid certain other truths. If she was bent on examining her own situation with the same sort of brutal honesty that she applied to all her other investigations, she would have to admit the real state of her heart. As if to remind her of its precarious position, that vital organ gave a little lurch.

Robbie would have to be informed that it hadn't happened at all like in the horrid novels. No clap of thunder, no swoon of joy had accompanied the momentous realization. Somehow, amid the snarls and the smiles, the confrontations and the closeness, love had simply . . . happened.

She didn't know whether to laugh or cry.

It was hardly the sort of story to inspire a novelist to lift a pen, she thought with a rueful grimace. Rather a playwright to compose a farce—

"Aurora!"

Her head came up, wondering who on earth could possibly be interrupting her thoughts.

"I thought it was you!" Jack reined his mount to a slow walk beside the carriage and tipped his hat with a gentlemanly flourish. "How wonderful to see you again, and under more comfortable circumstances." His broad grin shifted to include the others. "Good day, Woodbridge." He gave a polite nod to the older woman. "I'm afraid I have not had the pleasure . . ."

"Wheatley," murmured Alex in reply. "Then allow me to

introduce Miss Robertson. Robbie, this is Viscount Wheatley, eldest son of the Marquess of Sedge—"

"Good Heavens, was I the only one unaware that the entire House of Lords was rusticating in the North?" snapped
Aurora.

Jack colored slightly. "Your pardon for the little subterfuge, but when engaged in a clandestine mission—"

"Yes, yes, I know—when engaged in a clandestine mission, it doesn't do to reveal your true identity," she muttered.

"Er, what brings you here to Town," he asked quickly, in
an endeavor to change the subject. "I seem to recall you
mentioning that you never had occasion to visit."

"Some pressing matters of personal business have required my presence," she replied tightly.

"I see." As a gentleman, he forbore making further inquiry. "I do hope they are resolved to your satisfaction." He
adjusted the angle of his brim. "But how delightful to have
you here. Where are you staying?"

Keeping her eyes averted from Alex, Aurora gave a small
cough. "By purest chance, it was discovered that Lord
Woodbridge's great-aunt and I are related. Through marriage. Miss Robertson and I are residing for the next little
while at her town house while she is away in Bath."

"Splendid! You must promise to come to the gala ball my
mother is giving at Sedgewick House on Friday evening.
She has outdone herself in the preparations, and as she is ac-
corded to be one of the best hostesses in London, the
evening will no doubt be a stunning affair."

"Oh, b-but . . ." A *ball?* The chance to wear a frothy
gown? The prospect of waltzing in a gentleman's arms? She
had done neither in her life, and the very thought of it reduced her words to an incoherent stammer.

Jack looked a bit crestfallen at her less than enthusiastic
response. "Perhaps you do not care for such frivolous enter-

tainment, given some of your, er, opinions on human nature."

"No, it's not that. I-I am simply not sure we are free." Her eyes flew to Miss Robertson in mute appeal. "Are we, Robbie?"

It was Alex who answered. "I think it might be fitted in between the visit to Astley's and the arrangements to see *A Lady of Great Sensibility* at Haymarket," he said dryly. "We shall be delighted to attend."

"Wonderful! I shall have the invitations sent around to Woodbridge House." Seeing that the friends he had been out riding with were growing impatient for his return, he made to gather his reins and turn his stallion off the main way. "I'm afraid I must take my leave, but I look forward to Friday." His smile lingered on Aurora. "You must promise to save me a waltz."

"A waltz," repeated Miss Robertson, a dreamy expression softening her normally sharp eyes. "Imagine that!"

Aurora did just that, and the vision brought a particularly vile grimace to her features.

Alex's brows rose a fraction. "You truly dislike dancing?"

Still flustered by the turn of events, she blurted out, "I don't know how to dance!"

"So there is actually some discipline that you have not mastered?" He gave a low chuckle. "I thought all young ladies knew how to dance."

Color flooded to her cheeks. Stung by his teasing, a note of defensiveness crept into her tone. "It's all very well to laugh at my lack of feminine graces, sir," she said stiffly. "I am well aware of how unpolished I appear to you. But it's not as if I have had a great deal of opportunity to hone such skills."

The humor faded from his face. "You think I am making fun of you, Aurora?" he asked quietly.

Her mouth quivered at the sound of her name on his lips.

"I am well aware that you have had no chance to partake in the normal social activities befitting a lady of your station," he went on. "But not knowing how to execute a box step or a twirl may be rectified quite easily. I shall see that a dancing master comes to call at your town house daily. By Friday you will be leaving all the other young ladies in the dust."

Chapter Thirteen

As Aurora sailed by on the arm of yet another gentleman, Alex quaffed the rest of his champagne and somehow managed not to hurl the empty glass in her wake. He had wanted her to enjoy the evening, but not quite to this extent. *Damnation!* She had not missed one set yet, and by the look of the cluster of gentlemen gathered near her empty chair, it did not appear as if she would be sitting down anytime soon. The current tune had come to an end, but the violins were already striking up the chords of a waltz. He hadn't bothered stepping out onto the floor after the first few dances, but to avoid seeing the hand of some young buck come to rest at the small of her back, he turned on his heel and stalked off to refill his glass. Or, he reflected, maybe he should simply take up a whole bottle. He had a feeling he was going to need it.

His teeth set on edge. Perhaps it had not been the best of ideas to inform the fashionable modiste he had engaged for Aurora that her newest client needed a ball gown fit for a special occasion. Having all the measurements in hand,

Madame Mathilde had promised to deliver a work of art that would show off to perfection the charms of the lady in question. As his eyes strayed back to the froth of sea-foam green silk, and the vast expanse of creamy skin that it left uncovered, a low oath slipped from his lips. *Hell's teeth! If it showed any more of her charms, those lovely breasts would be bared for all to see!*

The thought caused a surge of heat to course through him that another glass of hurriedly consumed champagne did little to dampen. No doubt it had something to do with desire, for there was no denying that he ached to feel those soft curves cupped in his palms.

However, out of the corner of his eye he saw Aurora's partner pull her a fraction closer to his chest and he realized that desire did not answer for all that he was feeling. There was something else. Jealousy, perhaps? For right now his palms were also itching to be wrapped around the cursed fellow's throat for having the impudence to touch her in such an intimate way.

But the real source of the fire was something he couldn't quite put a finger on, since he had never experienced the sensation before.

As a scowl as black as his fine set of evening clothes came to his face, Alex sought to make some sense of the heat rising inside him. Why the devil did he care who danced with her? She was, he reminded himself, a most exasperating female—opinionated, disrespectful, and argumentative. Just because the sway of her slim hips and the sparkle in the depths of her emerald eyes caused him to want to sweep her up in his arms and carry her off to the nearest bedroom . . . A harsh sound, somewhere between a sigh and a groan, rumbled deep in his throat. It didn't help his mood any to suddenly realize he was still legally entitled to do just that!

Several gentlemen, on observing the Earl of Woodbridge's present expression, thought better of seeking to strike up a conversation, and caused their steps to swerve in a wide arc around him.

Damnation, he repeated once more, blithely unaware of the formidable face he was presenting. Retreating farther into the shadows cast by a towering arrangement of potted palms and exotic blooms, he turned and cast a glowering glance at the sea of swirling silks ebbing and flowing in tune with the lively music. It wasn't as if there weren't any number of ladies present who were far more beautiful—and far more willing to throw themselves into his arms.

The strange thing was, he didn't want anyone else but Aurora in his arms. In his bed. In his life.

Yet another long gulp of the sparkling wine slid down his throat. Alex stood for some time contemplating the spins and pirouettes of his own emotions; then his hand suddenly tightened around the glass with such force that the stem was in danger of snapping. Perhaps he had finally grasped hold of what had his senses so addled.

The word had four letters and began with an "L". . . .

It was lust, he tried to tell himself. But with a shake of his head, he had to acknowledge that what he was feeling was infinitely more complex than that, though lust was a part of its whole.

No, it was love that turned his life on its ear.

Alex slowly drained the rest of his drink, letting the import of the word seep into every fiber of his being. He might as well finally admit it, he told himself with a wry twitch of his lips. He loved Aurora, no matter the absurdity or the irony of it. Or the fact that she couldn't stand the sight of him.

The devil of it was, what was he going to do about it?

Aurora passed by yet again, this time with Jack ready to lead her out for the promised waltz. He watched the light of the myriad candles reflect off the silky curls framing her face. Like the young lady herself, the actual color seemed subtle, quixotic, and damnably elusive. Repressing a harried sigh, Alex set off in search of a waiter with a full bottle.

His steps took him past a cluster of turbaned matrons, their attention divided between keeping a basilisk eye on their charges and exchanging the latest salient tidbits of gossip. Off to one side, Miss Robertson sat by herself. Light winked off the lenses of her spectacles as she stared with rapt fascination at the glittering scene before her. Altering his direction, he drew to a halt beside her chair.

"Enjoying yourself, Robbie?"

She looked up, a sparkle evident in her eyes. "Very much, Alex. All the fine ladies and gentlemen in their elegant splendor, the chandeliers and the flowers, the music—it is even more wonderful than I ever imagined."

"No doubt you would enjoy it even more were you to join in the dancing yourself," he said softly as he extended his gloved hand.

Her jaw dropped. "Y-you can't mean to dance with . . . me?"

"Why not?"

"First of all, I'm an old woman! And secondly, that is a w-waltz that the musicians are preparing to play."

A smile played at the corners of his mouth. "First of all, I have noticed that for an 'old woman' you are still extremely agile. And secondly, I have it from a good source that you, too, know how to waltz since Aurora was in need of someone to practice with. So that seems to answer all the objections." Miss Robertson was drawn to her feet and the earl's arm came firmly around her ample waist.

After nearly treading on his toes for the first several steps, she appeared to compose herself and fell into the rhythm of the music, relaxing enough to follow his lead without the threat of doing him bodily harm. But after a series of box steps brought them to a less crowded spot on the dance floor, she looked up into his eyes with a searching gaze.

"Alex, if you do not mind, I have a rather pressing question I should like to ask you. Perhaps now is a good time, seeing as we have a chance to converse in a modicum of privacy."

A certain wariness shaded his reply. "Yes?"

"Why is it you are being so . . . nice to the two of us?"

The tightening of his jaw was barely perceptible in the flickering of the light. "So you, too, think me no more than an unprincipled rogue, acting out of some selfish desire to attain an end?" he asked softly. They turned, and a shadow danced across his face, making his expression even more inscrutable than before.

"Indeed not, sir." Her eyes didn't waver from his. "Actually I have become enormously fond of you, for I have come to the conclusion that you are no rogue at all, but rather a thoroughly nice gentleman. One who is intelligent, perceptive, and witty, as well as kind and compassionate."

For a moment he was speechless. Then a ghost of a smile flitted across his lips. "Are you flirting with me, Robbie?"

The older woman's cheeks turned a pink that matched the sash of her new gown. "Good heavens, am I?"

He chuckled. "Have a care, my dear. If I were available, I might be tempted to see just how serious you are."

They completed a series of twirls before she spoke again. "Are you not . . . available, Alex?"

Rather than answering right away, his brooding gaze sought Aurora among the other couples. He could swear that Jack's gaze kept sliding down to her cleavage.

"Kindly inform your charge that she is *not* to order any additional gowns from Madame Mathilde."

"I regret to inform you that in certain matters, I have absolutely no influence over Aurora."

His mouth quirked. "I can well believe it. Having spent a

week in my wife's company, I am more than aware of how deucedly mulish she can be!"

Behind the glint of her spectacles, Miss Robertson's eyes took on an appraising light. "And you would seek to drum such stubbornness out of her, sir?" she inquired.

There was a long pause. "Robbie, if I wanted a creature who obeyed my every command and answered to a cuff and sharp word, I would get a dog."

It was her turn to chuckle. "As I said, sir, you are a most enjoyable partner. Especially as your legs have remained quite steady throughout this dance instead of threatening to fold like an overdone soufflé."

Alex had to choke back a bark of laughter. Lord, he would miss this delightful woman almost as much as Aurora when it came time for them to quit London. "Are my legs to be a constant source of amusement to both of you?" he demanded, trying his hardest to sound aggrieved.

"Aurora has commented on your legs?"

"Indeed she has. Found them a subject for mirth as well. I believe she referred to them as great, hairy—er, that is . . ." To his acute mortification, he felt himself blushing like a raw schoolgirl.

Miss Robertson kept a straight face. "Well, she certainly has not mentioned finding fault with any other part of your anatomy."

He gave a strangled cough, then maneuvered her through a series of spins and turns, hoping that the quickened pace might help account for the fact that his cheeks were turning a shade redder. Finally regaining some mastery over his voice, he made an abrupt change of direction in the conversation as well. "Tell me, Robbie, does she truly find me as abhorrent as it appears?"

"Why do you ask, Alex?"

He drew in a deep breath. "Because I should like to know

whether she might consider tolerating my company for more than just the coming few weeks."

She took what seemed to him to be an inordinate amount of time to reply. "Hmm. Well, as to your question, Aurora insists that you are the most odious, insufferable, overbearing man she has ever met."

His face fell. "That bad?" Several more box steps were completed before he gave a rueful grimace. "So then, it would seem that I have no hope in the matter."

An unladylike snort escaped from his partner. "Come now, Alex! I would not have expected a seasoned military man to surrender so easily. Do you mean to tuck your tail between those long legs of yours—hairy or not—and slink off, leaving the field to someone else?"

Her gaze made a pointed shift to where Aurora was gliding along in the viscount's arms. Alex's eyes narrowed and his fingers clenched tighter around hers, but he said nothing.

"She might forgive the first desertion, you know," added Miss Robertson in a low whisper. "But I doubt she would look kindly on it happening again."

He grimaced. "But Robbie, if she hates me—"

"I can see that despite your experience in the ways of the world, you still have much to learn about females in general and Aurora in particular. Trust an old governess when I say that, like many situations seen in the heat of battle, things may not be as grim as they seem. You must simply come up with the right tactics to turn the tide in your favor."

His brow furrowed in thought. "Tactics, you say?" As he spoke, he looked once more in Aurora's direction, and to his eye it looked as though the space between her chest and Jack's elegant evening coat had lessened considerably. The pensive expression slowly turned into a scowl nearly as black as his friend's well-tailored garment.

"Yes, tactics. And as on the battlefield, you must be willing to take some risk in order to achieve victory." She cleared her throat. "And one other thing, Alex, if I may make so bold as to suggest an initial change in strategy. No lady in her right mind would feel encouraged to wax romantic over a gentleman who is constantly looking at her with such a glowering face."

"Face! What face? I am *not* making a face."

"Yes, you are. And a very odious one at that. Your brows draw together in a most forbidding manner and your lip curls up at the left corner."

The devil take it! It was clear that this campaign was going to be infinitely more daunting than facing off against Marshal Nye himself.

"You look absolutely divine this evening." As he spoke, Jack executed a skillful bit of footwork to avoid collision with an elderly gentleman whose partner looked to be as broad in the beam as a ship of the line. His grin then became even more pronounced. "And judging by the number of besotted gentlemen all but kneeling by your chair, you have converted more than your share of acolytes."

"I can't imagine what on earth has inspired such silly behavior."

"Can't you?" His brow arched up, but instead of answering directly, he went on in the same teasing vein. "I take it Woodbridge is reduced to squiring Miss Robertson about the floor because he didn't think to secure a spot on your dance card in advance. No chance now. He would need a regiment of foot soldiers to cut a path to your feet, even if there were a blank space left. Which there isn't."

"You may be sure the earl has not the least interest in stepping out with me," replied Aurora rather stiffly, taking great pains not to look in Alex's direction. That was certainly true enough, she thought—he had not so much as glanced her way the entire evening! His gaze had been riveted on the voluptuous raven-haired beauty whom he had partnered for the first waltz. Or, to be more specific, on the goodly amount of cleavage that the lady's low-cut burgundy gown showed off to perfection. Her eyes pressed closed for an instant, as if such action might also help banish the picture of how the lady's head had tilted back in soft laughter at something Alex had murmured close to her ear. And how dazzling his smile had been in return. To her dismay the threat of tears stung her lids.

Oh, what did it matter that he had held another woman in his arms? He would very soon have another wife in his life, and she should be well glad of it. Better to live with an aging governess and a calico cat than with a handsome husband whose sentiments would never match her own. Alex didn't love her, and the pain of knowing that his eyes—and his heart—could not help but wander would be unbearable.

She blinked once more and forced her attention back to her dance partner. "And of course, there is no reason for his lordship to ask for a set," she added with a shrug of unconcern. "Duty has obliged him to dance attendance on me quite enough over the past week. I imagine he is delighted to be free of the obligation, at least for an evening." So delighted, she added to herself, that he had rather dance with Robbie than consider asking for her own hand.

"Ah, yes," murmured Jack. "You did mention that you are related to his aunt. By marriage, is it?"

"Yes." Her mouth set in a grim line. "The connection is through marriage."

For a moment he was silent, a thoughtful expression on his features. "Hmm. That must make you related to Alex by marriage as well."

Aurora's foot jerked left when it should have slid right, causing her to come down rather heavily on his foot. "Oh, do forgive me, Jack," she gasped as he stifled a little yelp of pain. "I-I did warn you that I have very little experience in making my way in Polite Society."

"You are doing marvelously well," he reassured her with a game smile while trying not to limp too noticeably through the next series of turns. For a moment Aurora thought she had managed to change the direction of the conversation as well, but Jack's next words proved his curiosity was not so easily squashed as his toes. "I take it the two of you were not aware of your, er, relationship during the time in the North?"

She bit her lip. "His lordship and I had met only once before, a long time ago when I was but a child. My name, as well as my person, had changed in the meantime, and as he chose not to reveal his true identity, neither of us had the slightest inkling of the connection. It was only by merest chance that the truth came to light when I was summoned to London on . . . family business."

"A strange twist of fate," he said with a faint smile.

Ha! That was putting it rather mildly, thought Aurora to herself.

He gave a slight cough. "To return to the question of your new admirers—perhaps you should know that Lady Renfrew has let fall several interesting comments during the evening."

"Has she?" To her vast relief, Aurora recognized a flourish of notes that indicated the melody was nearing its end. "Well, I imagine one does not reach such an advanced age without having picked up at least one or two things that are worth listening to."

There was a flicker of amusement in his eyes. "Especially when one is a nosy old lady who makes it a point to learn every *on dit* that is repeated in Town. As a matter of fact, the topic of conversation was you—"

"Me!"

"A lovely lady with an aura of mystery about her—you may not be acquainted with the *ton*, but surely you understand human nature well enough to know how tantalizing that is. On top of that, Lady Renfrew has made it a point to mention that you have . . . expectations."

"Expectations?" she repeated faintly.

"Of coming into a generous settlement. And of seeking a husband." He cleared his throat. "She has dropped more than a few hints that Mr. Sprague is no more. Is that true?"

"Yes, Mr. Sprague has departed from this world," she answered through gritted teeth. "But I assure you that I am *not* seeking a new husband."

"Ah. Well, given your sentiments on the first one, I suppose that is not to be wondered at. Still, Lady Renfrew did say that—"

This time, Aurora sidestepped the issue with a bit more adroitness than before. "Surely you are too much of a gentleman to put much credence in gossip."

His mouth opened, then shut.

Seizing the advantage, she hurried on. "Oh look. I do believe that is Mr. Drimble, my next partner, who is waving at us." She made a show of consulting the card dangling from her wrist. "Yes, so it is."

"So it is." His expression became rather odd. "Forgive me. As a gentleman I should honor your reluctance to speak more on the subject. But as a friend . . ."

The arrival of the portly Mr. Drimble to claim Aurora's hand made further words impossible. With a gracious bow, Jack relinquished his place. He exchanged greetings with several acquaintances, but rather than linger in the crowded ballroom, he chose to wander out through the set of open French doors that led to the terrace. A breeze had blown out several of the torches, but as he leaned back against the carved marble balustrade, the remaining flickers revealed that he was not alone.

"You and your partner appeared to be enjoying yourselves immensely, Wheatley." Irritation bubbled up in

Alex's voice, though a surfeit of champagne submerged the worst of it.

Jack turned a quizzical eye on him. "Yes, well, Aurora is a most interesting—and unique—companion, as we both have reason to know," he replied lightly. "Never a dull moment in her presence." He watched a moth veer toward the nearest open flame, then shrugged as if acknowledging that his next actions might be equally as foolhardy. "Already she has no dearth of admirers, what with the intriguing little hints Lady Renfrew has let drop over the course of the evening. It appears the combination of her striking looks, the possible prospect of Fenimore blunt, and a healthy dash of mystery concerning her past have made her the most fascinating addition to the marriage mart in quite some time."

A muttered oath was the only reply.

"I imagine she will soon have a number of offers to sort through. Daunting task for a lady, especially one unacquainted with Society. But then, she has you to turn to for advice on whose suit to accept."

Despite the experience of several trips aboard a Royal Navy vessel, Jack felt his ears turn red at the rather lengthy string of curses that followed. He ducked his head and studied the fobs on his watch chain until the last of the invectives had died away. "Er, do I take that to mean you are not in favor of her contracting another match?" he asked with great innocence.

"You may take that to mean that regardless of what rumors you have heard, Aurora is not . . . available," growled Alex.

"I see. Well, she seems to be in complete agreement with you, though perhaps not for the same reason." He still had not looked up from the intricate intaglio designs cut into the bits of onyx. "And what of the other rumors I have heard? It's said by some at Whitehall that you are—well, that you are married, though no one seems to have ever met your wife. Or to have the slightest notion of whether she might be English, Spanish, Hindu, or Tartar."

Alex turned so that nothing was visible of his face save for a hard-edged profile silhouetted by a faint aureole of light from the closest torch. "We are discussing Aurora, not my personal affairs."

"The two aren't . . . related?" asked Jack softly.

The earl's jaw became even more clenched.

"Perhaps it is none of my business, but I have come to think of the two of you as friends. I have been told that marriage is an enviable state if one has chosen the right partner. The trouble is a mistake, once made—"

"Stubble it, Wheatley," replied Alex in what was clearly a tone of warning. "I am in no mood for any more advice this evening, especially from one who has spent the last quarter of an hour staring down the dress of the lady in question."

Jack looked as if he didn't know whether to laugh or to issue a challenge for the coming dawn. Then, stung by the earl's acid comment, he was moved to make his own sharp retort. "At least I have a right to stare at those lovely curves. I am able to offer her something more than a tap on the shoulder."

Alex's hand was suddenly clenching the intricate folds of the other man's cravat. "The devil you do!" he snarled, all his frustrations overflowing onto his friend. "I advise you to—"

The musicians must have taken a break from their playing, for several couples appeared on the edge of the terrace, and a murmur of voices indicated that others were not far behind. Alex's fingers slipped from the starched linen, leaving Jack to smooth at the crinkled folds, along with his own ruffled feelings.

"Have a care, Woodbridge," he said softly, shaking his head and regarding the earl with a measure of anger and sympathy. "I do not pretend to understand what is going on, but something tells me that it is more dangerous for both of you than anything we faced in Scotland. I shall not forgive you if you hurt her."

"Jack!"

Aurora was among the couples seeking a breath of fresh air, and on catching sight of her friend, she nearly dragged her latest escort away from one of the paths leading out to the gardens. By the twist of the fellow's features, it was clear that his intention in taking a walk had not been to share her company with other gentlemen. Still he had no choice but to accede to her wishes and reluctantly followed her lead over to the stone balustrade.

"Jack," she repeated. "Lord Greeley suggested a tour of your mother's garden, but I would much rather stay here and converse with friends." Her smile wavered slightly at catching sight of the figure behind him. "Good evening, Lord Woodbridge," she added a bit more hesitantly. "I do not wish to interrupt a private conversation—" Taking in the grim expressions of both gentlemen, she drew to an abrupt halt. "Is something amiss?" she asked.

"No, we have just finished on a subject that perhaps was a bit too serious to be discussed at an evening meant for fun and frivolity," replied Alex as he brushed a speck of pollen from his sleeve. "I trust you are having a pleasant evening, Mrs. Sprague?" he inquired with a cool politeness.

She nodded, though her own expression was hardly gay.

Her partner looked decidedly uncomfortable at having run smack into the nominal head of the lady's family. "Awfully warm inside," he stammered, eyeing the earl's muscled shoulders with some trepidation. "Mrs. Sprague remarked on how she would like to escape for a moment or two from such a crush. Er, hope you have no objection."

"Not at all." Alex had turned to pick up his glass, a shrug of nonchalance masking the urge to plant the spindle-shanked young man a facer he would not soon forget for keeping his hand resting on Aurora's wrist. "Mrs. Sprague is quite capable of making her own decisions. But I, on the other hand, am finding I have had enough of the chill night air. I think I shall go back inside and enjoy the rest of the festivities." Leaving a still-offended Jack, a slightly hurt Aurora and a vastly relieved Lord Greeley, he headed back toward the open French doors.

So much for a change in strategy, he thought, thoroughly disgusted with his own actions. He had nearly come to blows with a well-meaning friend and then managed no more than a scowl—no doubt an odious one—for Aurora. At this rate his campaign would be routed before it had properly begun. Perhaps he would be better off changing tactics and seeking out the sultry widow who had partnered him for the first waltz of the evening. She, at least, seemed able to tolerate his presence.

But instead of looking for solace in that direction, he merely drained another glass of champagne and gave orders for his carriage to be brought around.

"Well, Lord Woodbridge does not appear to be a fellow to kick up a dust over your activities, it seems," said Aurora's escort as he mopped at his brow with a silk pocket square and gave silent thanks for the earl's departure.

"No," she said quietly, her eyes surreptitiously following Alex's progress through the growing throng of revelers until he disappeared into the ballroom. "But I am not a green chit, without any experience in the world. There is no need for him to take any notice of what I choose to do."

Jack was watching her just as carefully. "You think Woodbridge does not care what you choose to do?"

"Why should he?"

"Why, indeed?" he said, so softly it was nearly inaudible.

"What lovely roses your mother has, Jack," Aurora said after a moment, abruptly taking hold of one of the lush stems growing up a fanned trellis. "Do you know its name?"

His lips quirked. "I believe it is called a wandering rose."

She essayed a tight smile. "Really? It seems quite at home here."

"Yes, well, some wanderers do indeed get lucky and find a spot that suits them."

Her escort fidgeted from one foot to the other. "Can't tell a dahlia from a daisy," he muttered.

Aurora gave a small shiver, then turned away from both the gentlemen and the flickering lanterns. "His lordship is right—the air has taken a decided chill to it. And in any case, I believe I hear the music beginning to start up. I had best be going in to meet my next partner."

He would, however, not be the partner she longed for.

Chapter Fourteen

Sick!" The heavy silk of her gown swooshed around her ankles as Aurora crossed the room in some haste. "Why, you are *never* sick."

"I am on occasion. If you will remember, I was sick when you decided to set out for Scotland." Miss Robertson pulled her wrapper tighter and took another sip of tea from the tray on her lap. "And as you keep so vociferously reminding me, you were able to manage everything quite well on your own. So I imagine that for a single evening, my company will not be missed." A mournful sigh followed. "Though I was *so* looking forward to the fireworks."

Aurora's eyes narrowed in some suspicion. "What a corker," she muttered under her breath as she began to pace before the hearth. "You hate loud noises."

"Ah, but I find I've become used to them over the last little while." Her former governess regarded her with a look of great innocence, then added a hacking cough for good measure.

"In that case, we could always postpone it to another time."

"That would be a rather churlish thing to do, as Alex has already gone to the trouble of arranging the trip, and will be arriving any minute now." Miss Robertson fiddled with the blanket covering her knees. "However, as it seems your nerves are all in a twitter about spending the whole evening alone with him, I suppose you may be allowed to cry off."

The pacing stopped and her chin came up in a stubborn tilt. "Don't be ridiculous! I am not the least affected by the prospect of his lordship's company—with or without your presence. After all, he and I have managed to put personal feelings aside and stick to our agreement to behave civilly to each other. This outing should prove no exception." She turned her back to the burning logs and tried to ignore the hiss and crackle of her own emotions at the idea of being together with Alex for hours, just the two of them. "The only explosions this evening will be of the gunpowder variety."

Miss Robertson ducked her head to hide a small smile. "Well, in that case, you might want to extinguish the sparks in your eyes."

Before she could fire off a retort, a discreet knock sounded on the door and the butler entered. "Lord Woodbridge has arrived."

Snatching up her shawl and reticule from one of the side chairs, Aurora made to quit the room.

"Why, aren't you going to invite him in for a glass of sherry before you set out?" asked Miss Robertson. "It's a rather long carriage ride out to Vauxhall Gardens."

Aurora's hand came to rest on her hip. "What?" she intoned with exaggerated surprise. "And run the risk of having the earl catch your catarrh?"

A prolonged fit of coughing followed. "Quite right. Well, do enjoy yourself, my dear."

Ha! Aurora arranged the folds of India silk over her bare

shoulders and restrained the urge to behave like an unruly schoolgirl and stick out her tongue at her former governess. The last thing she expected was to enjoy the coming outing!

But as she descended from the elegant carriage some time later, Aurora had to admit that so far, the evening was not proving nearly as dreadful as she had feared. In fact, the journey in close proximity with Alex had been quite pleasant and had passed almost too quickly. A bit of their former easy banter had been recaptured as they exchanged their various impressions of London, from the latest exhibit at the Royal Academy to the shops on Bond Street to the daily promenade of people in the parks.

Alex had appeared perfectly content to avoid all mention of personal matters. His manner was friendly but distant, and he seemed not to be the slightest perturbed at finding himself alone with her. Indeed, it was clear that her presence had no effect on him at all!

Lord, she wished the same might be said for herself. He looked so impossibly handsome in his elegant black evening clothes and starched linen that she hardly dared venture a glance in his direction, for fear of how easily he would see the true state of her feelings.

He offered his arm and escorted her to the private box he had reserved for their late supper. He pulled out her chair with a gallant flourish, then seated himself next to her, close enough that his thigh brushed up against hers with disquieting frequency. Shaved ham and champagne appeared, and the conversation continued to flow as freely as the sparkling wine. Why, Aurora could almost imagine that they were a normal married couple, out for a romantic evening under the stars.

So why did she feel that at any moment she was going to burst into tears?

Because, she reminded herself, this storybook chapter would soon come to an end. The pages would snap shut, proving that heroes and love and other such romantic non-sense were no more substantial than a thin coating of ink on paper. Her appetite suddenly deserted her and she merely sipped from her glass, wishing that the bubbly effervescence might have some effect on her depressed spirits.

Alex appeared not to notice her mood.

"Shall we take a stroll, sir?" She gestured to the graveled walks that led off to a section of the pleasure gardens that lay in deep shadows. "I imagine the fireworks would be even more visible in an area where there are not so many lights."

His mouth crooked in an odd smile. "The darkened paths of Vauxhall are considered a rather risky place for a lady to venture."

"Why is that?"

"They are infamous as a place where lovers meet and passions flare up with all the intensity of the display soon to take place overhead."

Aurora turned quickly so that he might not see the sparks of longing in her eyes. "Well," she said lightly, "there is lit-tle danger of me inspiring any strong emotion in your breast, sir, unless it is great relief that I will soon be gone from your life."

Alex said nothing, but tucked her arm more firmly under his and turned toward the looming shadows.

Other couples strolled in the same direction, but quickly disappeared among the labyrinth of trees and tall hedges. They soon found themselves alone and walked on for a bit in silence, save for the crunch of their own steps upon the deserted path. Perhaps on account of his words, Aurora was acutely aware of the heat emanating through the fine melton wool of his sleeve. It caused flames to flicker deep inside her and a small shudder to race up her spine.

"Is it too chilly here?" inquired Alex politely. "Do you wish to return to the box?"

"No," she lied. "I'm quite comfortable."

A jerk of her shoulders nearly belied her words as his fingers came up to adjust her shawl. This was madness, to let the merest graze of his touch set her afire, she told herself. With a quick tug at the knotted fringe, she caused his hand to fall away. "You needn't trouble, sir."

His eyes lingered on the considerable amount of bare flesh that her low-cut bodice revealed and it seemed that a glimmer of humor lurked within their sapphire depths "No trouble at all. I simply thought that as you are unused to Town fashion, you might require a little assistance in warding off the effects of the night air."

Lord, she was having precious little success in warding off the effects that his husky baritone was having on her person, for it was definitely not the night air that was causing a rosy flush to steal over every inch of exposed skin. Grateful that the dearth of lanterns masked her reaction, Aurora gave a slight toss of her curls. "I am not nearly so delicate as a proper London belle, sir, so it is unlikely that I will suffer any dire consequences from a brief walk on a mild evening."

They walked on for a few more steps before he spoke again "Have you enjoyed your stay in London?"

"Oh, yes!" The sharp tone of her previous words gave way to a wistful note. "Even more than I imagined. It has been nearly overwhelming, with so many new sights and experiences—"

"Such as Lady Sedgewick's ball? Did you enjoy that as well?"

"I did," she said softly. "I must admit, I have always had a silly, schoolgirlish desire to attend such a grand fete." A wry grimace flitted across her face. "And thanks to your thoughtfulness, I managed not to make a complete cake of myself with my appearance or my footwork. I-I should have been mortified if I had put either you or Jack to the blush by revealing how out of place I really was."

"With a gown like that, you had little need to worry that any gentleman would seek to find fault with you," he replied dryly. "And you danced very well. But then again, you had a good deal of practice, for I don't believe you sat down for even one set."

Aurora blinked several times. "I am amazed you noticed anything about my activities," she said without thinking. "Your attention seemed to be engaged elsewhere."

It was his turn to look surprised.

"She was wearing burgundy, and you appeared to be intoxicated by the sight."

"Ah. Lady Talbot." He paused to smooth a crease in his cravat. "I knew her in Calcutta. Her husband passed away from a tropical fever six months ago and she has only recently returned to England."

"How very convenient. No wonder you had little desire to waltz with anyone else—" Aurora bit off the rest of her words and turned away, her face flooding with embarrassment. How could she have blurted out such a stupid thing?

Alex looked startled, then amused. "Are you perchance a touch . . . jealous?"

"J-jealous?" To her dismay, the scoff came out as little more than a squeak. "Don't be a-absurd! Of course I was not—" Her throat suddenly became so tight that further speech was impossible.

Alex had come to an abrupt halt and his hand had slipped to the small of her back, pulling her around to face him. His eyes seemed to have taken on a strange glitter. "No?" he whispered close to her ear. "Well, I was sorely tempted to plant Jack a facer on seeing him take you up in his arms."

Aurora found she could only stare at him in mute disbelief.

The faint strains of music drifted out on the zephyr of a breeze and suddenly Alex took up her hand. "Come, you have reminded me that we have never danced together, madame wife." He spun her in a slow circle, throwing her senses so off-kilter that the ground seemed to be moving in an altogether different direction than her body. A wave of dizziness washed over her, along with the bemused realization that for the first time in her life, she might actually discover what it was like to be in need of a strong whiff of vinaigrette.

As if sensing the danger, his arms tightened, forcing her legs to straighten and her chin to come up. Their eyes met, and for an instant, all she was aware of was the exact shade of his eyes, and how much she would miss every subtle curve and contour of his countenance, even the irritating little arch of his brow and twist of his lip when he was annoyed with her.

With a stifled cry, she tore her gaze away and stared out into the murky shadows. That was what the future held, she reminded herself. Nothing but a drab darkness, devoid of any sparkle or color. Most especially any hue remotely resembling sapphire blue.

To her relief, Alex seemed no more inclined to speak than she was. There was silence, save for the gentle rustle of the leaves and the sliding rhythm of their steps. Recovering some measure of composure, Aurora sought to savor the rest of the waltz. It was highly unlikely she would ever have a chance to repeat the experience, so it was best to concentrate on remembering every last detail—the feel of his gloved fingers entwined with hers, the subtle scent of bay rum and leather, the touch of—

Her experience with balls and waltzes was, she knew, exceedingly limited, but even so, she knew enough to sense that his thighs were suddenly pressing much too close for propriety. A moment later, they were molded hard up against hers, his rising desire impossible to deny. As her bodice was crushed against the lapels of his coat, she opened her mouth to murmur some sort of protest.

His lips came down hard upon hers as the first rocket exploded in the sky. The thunderous bang drowned out her cry of passion and his answering groan. A shower of sparks lit up the sky, but the display was nothing in comparison to the pyrotechnics taking place between them. Set afire by the heat of his kisses, she cried out again, then melted into him.

"Sweeting," he said in a hoarse murmur. "Ah, sweeting." His mouth trailed down the swell of her breast and closed hungrily over the thin silk covering her nipple.

Aurora gave a muffled gasp at the burst of pleasure that shot through her insides. Lost to all reason, her fingers began to wreak havoc on the precise folds of his cravat as they fumbled with the gold studs of his shirtfront. One of them fell to the ground, allowing her hand to slip inside the fine linen and splay against his bare chest. "Oh, Alex," she whispered, her palm brushing over the dark curls. This might be madness, she knew, but she could no more douse the flames of her need than she could stop the rain of sparks in the heavens above.

His head came up at the sound of his name. She said it again, and all at once they were locked in another passionate embrace, clinging to each other as if they could somehow grab hold of all the time they had missed together.

Eyes ablaze, Alex stopped his kisses long enough to lift her up against the nearest tree. His mouth then sought a more torrid intimacy as he straddled her legs and began to ruck her skirts up past her knees.

Aurora arched back, savoring the wickedly wonderful feeling of being wanted by a man. And not just by any man, but by Alex. If she was not grossly mistaken, what was about to happen was not so different from one of the illustrations in his well-traveled little book, and anticipation simmered up inside her. *Spicy indeed!* She kneaded the corded muscles of his shoulders, thinking she would not mind a steady diet of Indian fare. Surely it was not so very wrong to

hunger for his ambrosial kisses and whispered endearments.
He was, after all, still her lawfully wedded husband.

A bittersweet smile stole to her lips as she reached down
to help him with the fastening of his breeches. Perhaps it
was only for a short while longer, but in the meantime—

A group of drunken young bucks stumbled out from
around a tall privet hedge. A titter of laughter shattered her
reverie, followed by more than a few ribald comments. It
seemed like an age to her before their steps retreated back
toward another path as they called out more lewd suggestions, ones that made clear exactly what sort of female they
thought she was.

Aurora broke away with a strangled sound somewhere
between a laugh and a sob. Indeed, what else *could* they
think of a female who had been about to let a man toss her
skirts in the bushes of a public venue? Her hands came up
over her cheeks and she was dismayed to find they were
burning hotter than a Madras curry. Good Lord, she hardly
knew what to think of herself! Why, since meeting Alex, it
was as if she had become an entirely different person from
the steady, sensible Aurora Sprague she had been all her life.

And what was he thinking? Was it his opinion, too, that
she was no better than a lightskirt? Is that what had whetted
his appetite?

The very thought cut through her like a knife.

"I-I think it best if you take me home immediately, sir,"
she said in an unsteady voice, turning her back as much to
hide her confusion and embarrassment as to attempt to put
some order to her disheveled clothing.

It was of some consolation to see that Alex appeared as
shaken as she was. His hand raked through his tousled locks
and his jaw betrayed a slight tremor as he made several attempts to speak. Finally, after a harried sigh and some fum-
bling to reknot his cravat and retrieve his stud, he merely
gave a curt nod. "As you wish."

Holding her hand, he guided her back to where the carriages waited, taking great care to skirt the more populous areas, where a crowd still lingered. He paused only long enough to give a terse order to the coachman before helping her up into the darkened interior. As soon as the door was pulled closed, the whip snapped in the air, signaling the horses to spring forward.

Hell's teeth, he cursed. Had he really behaved like a randy donkey and tried to mount his wife in the middle of Vauxhall Gardens? She must truly think him an ass! No—she must think him a louse! Alex leaned his head back against the squabs, thankful that the interior lamps had been left unlit and the curtains were still drawn, so that his grimace of self-loathing was hidden from view.

So much for tactics and strategy, he thought glumly. Had he still been in the army, such a cowhanded blunder would have resulted in his carcass being left as pickings for the vultures. It did little to improve his frame of mind to think that once Robbie got through with him, his fate might be exactly the same.

The darkness, though it served as a welcome cloak to cover his own emotions, made it impossible to discern Aurora's expression. She had settled in the opposite corner, as far away from his person as possible. Not even the hem of her skirt brushed against him and her head was turned toward the door, despite the lack of a view.

May Lucifer be roasted! He could only imagine what she was thinking.

A moment of further reflection brought the slow realization that he couldn't possibly imagine what she was thinking. Nor, he added with an inward wince, would he want to.

His own thoughts were bad enough.

Not only had he lost any chance of winning her regard—

not to speak of her heart—but he had botched it in such an unforgivable manner. He fell to massaging his temples. A straw pallet could, he supposed, have been forgiven, considering the circumstances. But if he were going to attempt to seduce his own wife a second time, why the devil hadn't he done it in the proximity of shimmering candlelight, crisp linen sheets, and a well-padded bed?

It was what she deserved, to have her glorious limbs stretched out on the wide expanse of his carved tester bed. *Their* carved tester bed. At least it was for a little while longer. *Damnation!* He gave a silent oath as the realization washed over him that he didn't *have* to seduce her. He could have simply carried her up to his own comfortable bed-chamber.

It suddenly occurred to Alex that he was an idiot as well as a louse.

His thoughts were still running in such a depressing direction when they reached the cobbled streets of Mayfair. For a moment he nearly lost his nerve and considered abandoning his original plan. There were limits to how much of a fool a gentleman wished to appear in the course of a single night, even a gentleman in love. But then, with a wry purse of his lips, he decided there was really nothing to lose by going on with it. How could he sink any lower in her estimation? Besides, Robbie would likely send someone to chop his shaking legs off at the knees if he lost his courage and made a cowardly retreat.

The carriage came to a halt. Alex threw open the door and helped Aurora down. She blinked several times, just as much from confusion as from the need to adjust her eyes to the flickering streetlights after the pitch-black of the carriage interior. For the first time since leaving Vauxhall Gardens, she spoke.

"W-where are we?" she demanded in a tight whisper as she stared up at the imposing town house. "This is not—"

Alex took hold of her hand and started up the polished stone steps. "Please, it will only take a moment. There is something inside that . . . belongs to you. I would like for you to have it now, tonight, before you rush off back to your calico cat and distressed females."

Leaving me an even more distressed gentleman, he added to himself.

She bit her lip, but followed along without further protest. Alex whisked her through the half-opened door and across the arched foyer before the startled butler could blurt so much as a simple greeting. Their hurried steps echoed down an imposing corridor lined with gilt-framed portraits, until he finally drew her off to the right and into a small wood-paneled study.

"What is this place?" she asked again, the words hardly audible as her gaze took in the shelves of leather-bound books, the expensive Oriental carpet, and the marble hearth, decorated with a detailed carving of entwined acanthus leaves.

His eyes finally met hers, their sapphire color alight with a strange glimmer. He was, he realized, more nervous than if he had been facing a thousand screaming, charging, knife-wielding Pashtu rebels bent on carving him into little pieces to float down the Ganges. Against such an attack he might fight back. Against Aurora he was defenseless—with a word she could slice his heart to ribbons.

"This is Woodbridge House," he answered softly. "You said to take you home."

Aurora went very pale. "I—you—" Overcome with confusion, she quickly looked away. "W-what was it you wanted me to have, sir? How can there be anything here that is mine?"

Without answering, Alex took a small leather box from the top drawer of his desk. He opened it, hesitated for a moment, and then held it out to reveal what was inside. Lying on a fold of velvet was a ring of exquisite craftsmanship, the design simple but beautifully wrought. Centered in the gold detailing was a flawless emerald, flanked by two sapphires.

"I bought the sapphires in India because they seemed a kindred stone to me," he explained. "For some reason, the emerald caught my eye as well. It seemed . . . a good match. The colors complemented each other—different shades, but of the same family." He drew in a rather ragged breath. "Y-you may think of it as a reminder of our brief time together. A part of me shall always be with you, even if I am not there in person." As he spoke, he extended his palm. "It also occurred to me that I have never given you a wedding gift."

She made no effort to take it. In fact, her arms clasped around her chest and she turned around to face the banked fire. The gesture caused a small stab to knife through his insides.

"I know you think me a complete cad." He let his arm fall back to his side. "Lord, I have more faults than most men. I have been selfish, cowardly, and callous to name but a few of them—I am sure you would have no trouble adding to the list, especially after my behavior tonight . . ."

A loud sniff interrupted him.

"Aurora, might you turn around?" he pleaded. "Much as I enjoy the sight of your lovely shoulders, I shall never find the courage to finish the rest of what I want to say if it's clear you loathe me so much that you can't bear to look at me."

Ever so slowly, she moved to face him, though her eyes remained glued to the tips of her slippers.

Alex hadn't realized that he had been holding his breath until it came out in a rush of relief. Swallowing hard, he dared go on. "It was as if I had been wandering in the dark until our paths crossed. You made me look at myself—and a good many other things—in a whole new light. I meant to try to make up for some of my transgressions. The reason I sought out my wife was so that I might make some sort of amends for my unforgivable neglect by granting her the freedom she deserved." He paused. "And so that I might be free to seek you out. I don't know what I meant to do about Mr. Sprague, but I would have figured out something. Perhaps carried you off to India. You would, by the way, find it a most fascinating place . . ." He realized he was babbling and yet couldn't seem to stop. "I meant to offer you the ring as soon as the Runner located your whereabouts, but if you don't like it—"

Tears were flowing down her face. "Like it?" She wiped at her cheeks with the backs of her hands. "I—I love it."

"Did you say the word 'love'?" *Perhaps there was hope.*

"You heard me—I love the ring."

"Ah, the ring." *Well, it was a start.*

"Yes, I love the ring. And I love the way your eyes reveal just as many facets as the cut gems. I love your courage, your strength, your sense of humor. I even love the annoying little wiggle of your brow when you are angry. Hell's bells, I love *you*, Alex Fenimore. Surely you must have realized that my heart was yours from the moment you fainted dead away in my arms."

An incredulous smile started to spread across his face. It turned to one of pure joy when she crossed the space between them and brushed a light kiss over his lips.

"I was praying that a certain barnyard animal might once again become airborne," he murmured before taking her in his arms. The kiss that followed had a sweet, haunting tenderness, rather than the hard, burning passion of earlier in the evening.

When finally he broke it off, Alex took her face between his hands and slowly traced his lips over the path her tears had left.

Such caresses only caused the drops to flow again. "Oh dear, I am never such a watering pot," she murmured between sniffles. "I may have need of that deuced bottle of vinaigrette yet."

He smiled, then ran his thumb along the ridge of her cheekbone. "Why the tears, sweeting?"

"It's just that . . . Robbie and I must soon return home, and then I shall probably never see you again."

"This is your home, Aurora. As you have noticed, it is a large place, with more than enough room for Robbie, an aged cook, a hobbled housekeeper, and a calico cat." He kissed her forehead. "And since your former governess will no longer be required to keep an eye on you, we will make sure she does not become too bored by having her teach our children to be as wonderful as their mother."

"B-but what about the annulment proceedings? The papers have been filed—"

With a roguish grin, he took the stack of foolscap that was sitting on the corner of his desk and tossed it into the fire. "Case dismissed."

Deciding he may as well consign his pride to the flames too, he dropped to one knee. "Never thought I would be brought to this by *any* female. But you've done it. Not through manipulation, or seduction, but by your compassion, your courage, your warmth, and your laughter. Dearest Aurora, my life will be eternally black as the deepest midnight hour if you are not there to be my shining light. Will you be my wife? This time in more than a mere sham of a marriage."

She dropped to her knees beside him. "We have both been humbled by our pride in thinking we were content in facing the world alone. Oh, Alex, I want more than anything to be your wife—"

He cut off the rest of her words with a thorough kiss. "You do?" he asked some minutes later.

"I do." She gave a mischievous smile. "But this time around, now that I have said the fateful words, I trust the shock of it won't cause you to cast up your accounts in the nearest vase."

He laughed, then spent a goodly amount of time proving that her presence was eliciting a far different physical reaction from him than a queasy stomach.

"You know," he murmured as he nibbled at the lobe of her ear, "there is something to be said for proposing to one's wife. I don't have to suffer through the delay of having the banns read, the interminable round of engagement parties, or the fuss of an elaborate ceremony. I can, in good conscience, carry you upstairs to our bedroom this instant. Which is exactly what I intend to do."

"Mmm. You truly wish to have and to hold me?"

His eyes were sparkling as he swept her up into his arms. "'Til death do us part."

Aurora leaned her head against his chest. "Well, amen to that, Alex Fenimore."

Signet Regency Romances from Allison Lane

"A FORMIDABLE TALENT...
MS. LANE NEVER FAILS TO
DELIVER THE GOODS."
—*ROMANTIC TIMES*

To order call: 1-800-788-6262